# Orbs of Purpose

## And Other Fantastical Stories

# Nicholas Licalsi

STEP INTO THE ROAD

From this point on take everything with a grain of sale. I made most of it up!

For Ollie and Evy, my nephews, I hope these short stories encourage you to explore any and all fantastical worlds you find out there.

# Thank You Patrons!

Your generous and lasting support encouraged me from the oldest stories in here to the newest.

Katelyn Combs, Bonnie, BW, Melinda Callender,
Roy & Beth Shockey, Callen McMillian, Sam Meeks, John Middleton.

# Contents

# Aldren's Abandoned Station

Published December 1, 2023 - StepIntoTheRoad.com

Feldman's Station was quiet despite it being Elder's Day. The once-crowded station had, like most of the Central System, cleared out. They hadn't gone anywhere in particular, but like humanity as a whole began to disappear, falling prey to the beasts humanity had awoken.

Aldren, a teenage girl with matted-haired and a patched-up jumpsuit that smelled like an algae vat left to grow on its own, had made Feldman's Station her home.

Or at least the parts of it that hadn't been sealed up due to breaches in the hulls. Those sectors had lost atmosphere and let in the deathly vacuum of space. Or worse, the things that lingered there.

Aldren couldn't leave Feldman's if she wanted to. The last ship had left months ago. It had carried a small crew of nomadic humans who jumped from outpost to outpost looking for surviving humans.

Feldman's was a common stop on those trips. It'd been famous for ages, popular enough to show up on the most outdated of nav systems.

Aldren was celebrating Elder's Day in style. She'd booked a table at Sunflower's Muse, one of the nicest restaurants still in atmo.

It wasn't hard to get a table.

The difficult part was finding a suitable meal. Anything fresh had molded before Aldren was born. The hydroponic vats still grew plenty of algae, but algae stew, chili, or soup was not a meal fit for Elder's Day. Most freeze-dried meals had been pillaged by Aldren and others who traveled to the station, leaving the already thin reserves dry.

But residents, former residents, of Feldman's Station had stashes. Aldren had sorted through countless bedrooms, personal belongings, and prized valuables. Most of which were useless to Aldren, hence why they were still on the station.

But in a nook under a bed, a freeze-dried ration had fallen and been forgotten. Until Aldren rescued it.

The vacuum-sealed zip t'lock foil bag was filled was beef stroganoff. Aldren hadn't had real beef and she didn't expect that to be changing today. This packet certainly held the vegan beef substitute.

Aldren poured the dried noodles, beef, and sauce flakes into a shallow white bowl. She'd picked this one out because it had the least number of chips in it. She poured hot water over the food to rehydrate it.

The room was immediately filled with the savory smell of beef and rich mushroom and onion sauce. A massive improvement from the salty green vegetable smell of algae chili.

Aldren listened to the Elder Day tunes she'd programmed into the station's public address system. The songs were upbeat and celebratory And would stick in your head for days after hearing them.

Other tables in the restaurant were set with muted yellow tablecloths and green napkins folded like hats. It'd taken a full day to do that, but Aldren wanted to keep the illusion that she wasn't alone on Elder's Day.

A present, wrapped in crinkled but shiny tin foil, sat across from Aldren. It stood out on the yellow tablecloth. She'd found something else useful in her pursuit of a good meal. And wrapped it for herself.

The beef stroganoff would take time to rehydrate. The best way to pass that time was to open the present.

Aldren carefully peeled back the plastic electrical tape, she didn't have much left. She unfolded the crinkled foil, which likely couldn't be used for much more in its life, but you don't survive on an abandoned space station by wasting supplies. The small cardboard box was easy to open. Aldren hadn't wasted tape keeping it closed.

She pulled out a mismatched pair of neon socks. They were long like a tube. One was pink with a blue patch on its toe and heel, the other was blue with a pink patch on the toe and heel.

The socks were absolutely gorgeous! Exactly what Aldren wanted.

She wrapped her arms around her chest and gave herself a warm hug. Another thing you had to do if you wanted to survive on an abandoned space station.

The stroganoff was as hydrated as it would be. Aldren knew there'd still be crunchy dehydrated bits in it. But that was the charm of freeze-dried meals, algae stew had no texture.

As she stirred the stroganoff around the public address system announced: "New ship docked in sector gamma partition C door 12."

Aldren had wired the station's security into the PA to keep from having to go through vacuumed sectors to access the station's security office. She'd also programmed the security feed to transmit directly to her hand terminal.

Aldren's heart sank. Unfortunately, she had guests for Elder's Day.

You don't survive long on an abandoned space station by getting excited about having company.

Sector gamma was mostly still in atmo. Lucky for the new ship. Some travelers docked into vacuum, no lack of hassle.

On Aldren's hand terminal, a feed of the sector gamma's security camera played. The image was focused on the door the ship docked to. The ship itself was ocean blue, not that Aldren had ever seen a real ocean. Harbor Master was painted in blocky white letters on the side. The ship as a whole was sleek like a knife or pair of needle nose pliers.

It was probably designed to land on planets and had to get through the heat of a planet's atmosphere.

Apparently, the operator of the Harbor Master was also not eager to have company. They hadn't opened the doors of the dock or made an appearance in the station yet.

Or if they had the cameras had missed it.

Another thing Aldren didn't appreciate.

An abandoned station had no security team to actively prevent hacking the camera feed. The simple security measures that Aldren could put in place were outdated and easy to bypass.

She took a bite of the stroganoff. She looked around and appreciated the neat grid of tables she'd laid out together in Sunflower's Muse. Keeping one eye on the terminal and another on her spoon, not wanting to spill a bite, she did her best to enjoy her Elder's Day meal.

If Aldren's visitor wasn't eager to see her, then she wasn't eager to see them.

Besides, not every human that visited Feldman's was friendly. But the station's booby traps would keep them out of Aldren's living quarters.

A snap rang through the Sunflower's Muse. It sounded like a circuit breaker blowing. Aldren dropped her spoon and splattered sauce all over the yellow tablecloth.

The smell of ozone, another clear sign of an electrical problem, filled the room.

Aldren grabbed her socks off the table. A fire in her station could be deadly. She knocked her chair over in her haste and turned around to make it to the door.

Unfortunately, a large toothy beast blocked her path.

The Awakening, caused by greedy Central System scientists if you believed the myths, let monsters into this universe through the space between space.

Some monsters were like whales and swam through the void of space swallowing ships whole. There were jellyfish-like creatures orbiting suns and placing their tentacles on the hot stars when they were hungry and casting the whole solar system into darkness once they were full.

The creature in front of Aldren had fur as black as the void of space. It stood on four legs and had triangular feline ears.

It seemed like a jungle cat, maybe a panther. And just like she'd seen in VR videos this panther had a short muzzle, muscular shoulders that reached Aldren's chest, and four tails that floated behind it.

Except Aldren didn't think panthers were supposed to have bulbs on the end of their tails. These bulbs, which only existed on three of the four hovering tails, twisted open like a flower blooming. Each was filled with an array of suction cup-like tendrils. Then they closed in the reverse motion, only to repeat the cycle a moment later.

On second thought, Aldren wasn't sure that panthers were supposed to have four tails at all.

"Hello," the panther said in a deep voice that seemed to shake the whole station. "What do you have there?"

The panther's yellow eyes with their inhuman vertical slits gazed at the socks in Aldren's hands.

Aldren buried the socks in the pocket of her jumpsuit.

"Nothing," she said rushed.

She had no gun, those were dangerous on a station. A multitool was strapped to the work belt of their jumpsuit, but the small blade would be as useful as the stroganoff-covered spoon.

"It's Elder's Day for you humans. Is it not?" the panther asked.

"Mhmm," Aldren said nervously. She backed away, uneager to get within paw's reach of the beast.

The beast kept up with Aldren's retreat. For every few steps back she took the panther caught up with a single stride.

Beasts like this didn't get the label of monster by being kind to humans.

"Isn't it tradition to give gifts to others on Elder's Day?" the panther asked.

"Of course," Aldren responded. "You can have..." she looked around the room and snatched a neatly folded green napkin off of a nearby table. "...this," she said holding the gift out.

The panther frowned, as much as a feline-faced extra-dimensional being could frown.

"There's no love or warmth in that gift," the panther complained.

"I folded it myself. For you," Aldren said. She pinched and pulled the edges making sure the folds were sharp and neat.

"They didn't want to give me a gift on the Harbor Master either," the panther said.

Aldren hummed in interest and concern for herself.

"They shot at me, trapped me, lopped off part of my tail."

The panther lowered the three tails that had pulsing bulbs on the ends. It was clear to Aldren that the fourth one had been cropped a bit short.

"But there was warmth and love in the family's ship. So I kept that as a gift. And I kept its course. Which led me to this station."

The panther smiled the kind of cruel smile a pirate would make in VR movies.

"Should I take this station from you?" the panther asked.

"No, no, no. You don't need to do that." A nervous laugh was clearly in her voice.

"There's no warmth in it either," the panther said sounding resigned.

Aldren agreed, hence why she wanted the socks. She dug them out of her jumpsuit. Sad to see the mismatched pink and blue tubes go.

One of the panther's tails reached out and grabbed them with the bulbous end.

"Thank you," the panther said.

With a snap like a circuit breaker and the smell of ozone, the cat disappeared.

Aldren sighed in relief and disappointment.

At least she still had her stroganoff.

And she knew you don't survive alone on an abandoned space station by arguing with extra-dimensional panthers.

# Field Guide for Kremulons

Published November 4, 2022 -
StepIntoTheRoad.com

I found it lying in the sand, a bright red, blue, and orange. If I returned it to my parents who were a few paces back maybe they could reunite the toy with its owner. If I let my brother Stevie see it he'd claim it as his own, then start tearing it apart.

It looked like a submarine, something to play with in the bath. It made sense that it was on the beach. Some kid a few years younger than me likely wanted his bath toys with him then forgot this one in the sand.

Then the bugs crawled out.

I stumbled back. I hate bugs. Stevie has a collection of plastic bugs that he hides around the house and scares me with. I should get over it, that's what dad always tells me to do, but I can't. Mom got me a book about birds because they eat bugs. I love birds now, but I still don't have the courage to face Stevie's bugs.

These bugs had six appendages but they only used their back two legs to walk. They looked unlike any insect Stevie had thrown at me.

Their skin was a vibrant turquoise like the breast of a bay-headed tanager and they had a bland sand-colored appendage that sat inside a translucent dome. A half dozen of them came out climbing down a ladder-like structure on the hull of the submarine.

"We've come to take over your planet, human," one of the bugs said to me.

This wasn't the first time a bug talked to me. Stevie gave the bugs voices all the time. They usually said something just as ridiculous and aggressive. However, this time the bugs weren't in Stevie's hands; he was down the beach kicking waves and throwing shells into the ocean. So I took a closer look at these tiny creatures.

"We are Kremulons from Kremu and this planet will soon become ours." Its voice was high pitched and garbled like they were speaking through a kazoo.

Stevie usually had that opinion about whatever toy I was playing with. I found it was best to let him have it for a bit until he got bored with it. I doubted these Kremulons would get bored of Earth as quickly.

"We could always share it?" I offered. A tactic that often failed to impress my brother but might be enticing to a more intelligent species.

"Your atmosphere is noxious to us and we plan to replace it with the methane we breathe."

I was familiar with filling the air with methane. My brother did what he called a "Dutch oven" and stuck my head under the covers while farting. So I knew methane was not an acceptable substitute for oxygen.

"Why do you want to live on Earth?" I asked.

There were countless planetary bodies in this solar system alone. I don't see why they had to have ours. I never understood why the thing I had was the most interesting thing in the world.

"Why not try filling Venus or Mars with methane?" I suggested.

"Because you've already begun the process to prepare for our arrival," the head Kremulon replied.

"You're not very big, I'm sure we could find a way to live together. You could live in our walls like a brownie."

"The Kremulons are a proud and numerous species. We are 50 billion strong and cover every square meter of Kremu. We will do the same here."

"It is insulting that you would offer us the useless remnants of your dwellings," another Kremulon said now holding something in his hand. Its bright paint job made it look like a miniature Nerf gun. A small red laser bolt launched out of it and hit my wrist.

"Ow!" It hurt, but wasn't as painful as a turn burn on my wrist from Stevie.

"We'll need to bring the higher-powered artillery in our second wave of ships," the Kremulon said.

"I'm including it in our reports," a third Kremulon replied while he wrote something onto a tiny notepad.

"I don't need any more artillery than my sandal," I replied.

"Are you threatening us?" the lead Kremulon asked.

"The reports of their telecommunications indicate they are a brutish and aggressive species." The Kremulon with the notepad said.

"It wasn't a threat," I backpedaled. "I'm just saying, maybe we should try and work something out."

"Kremulons did not become the most numerous species on Kremu by negotiating with beasts. We have tamed the towering multi-toothed tigers on the Timerion peninsula. We eradicated the poisonous balton plants that infested our grain fields. And we eliminated the exponentially multiplying Lowery locusts."

"And we're the brutish ones?" I scoffed.

"Each of those species and all the others we've mastered have shown aggression towards us. It was out of self-preservation."

"And what have humans done? I haven't even touched your ship." I could have thrown it into the ocean. It's what Stevie would have done.

"Based on our surveys of your species, there is no doubt that, given knowledge of another sapient species in your vicinity, you would stop at nothing to eradicate us. So we must be the first to strike."

"That doesn't sound good."

"Not for you," the Kremulon with the Nerf-like gun said.

"It could be a problem for you as well. The resplendent quetzal of Central America can eat a diverse number of foods like fruit, insects, and even frogs. That diversity helps it when certain foods are less plentiful. As a whole, the rainforest thrives because of its diversity."

"Outer space is a dark forest, not a rainforest," the Kremulon leader said.

"But does it have to be? A diversity of species could help both of us. You're using paper notepads while we have computer tablets that you could learn about. We could trade that for your ability to travel through space quickly."

"You want us to give you our most advanced technology so you can go find our planet and wipe us out?" the armed Kremulon said.

"We'd obviously have to agree not to wipe each other—"

"Whatcha got here, Tweety Bird?" The voice sent a shiver down my spine. Stevie was done tossing seashells into the ocean.

"Nothing." The word came out too quickly to be believable.

The submarine-shaped spaceship already had his attention. He lifted the multicolored toy up and tapped on it in a few places. It let out a hollow ring.

"Put that down," a Kremulon said.

"I don't think I will, Tweety Bird."

"You should probably put it down," I said knowing he wouldn't take my advice.

"Ow! Are you pinching me?" He looked down to find all the Kremulons shooting their Nerf-like guns at him. He easily blocked the incoming shots with the Kremulon ship.

"Those are some bright crabs," Stevie said.

"They're not crabs, they're aliens."

"Aliens are supposed to be scary like Predator. I watched that at Tommy's sleepover and wasn't even scared. I could crush these guys under my foot."

"You shouldn't do that." If he did, it would wipe out all my attempts to negotiate with them. Unfortunately, Stevie always loved pulling the bottom brick out of my block towers.

"Put our ship down," the Kremulons demanded. "Or we'll send word to the main fleet on Kremu of your species' aggression."

"Oh so you're a tattle tale," Stevie said. "Tweety Bird knows what I do with tattle tales."

Stevie kicked a pile of sand over the Kremulon crew and stomped on the pile he made. I heard glass crack.

"Come on Stevie, that wasn't very nice!" I said.

"I was getting tired of them pinching me. Now let's see if this thing floats!"

"That could be really important. We should give it to Mom and Dad." I reached for the bright ship.

"Nah, I don't think I'm going to do that!" Stevie said, rushing towards the waves.

I walked towards the umbrella my mom and dad sat under. I hoped they had my rainforest birds wildlife guide so I could read instead of play with Stevie. I also hoped that next time the Kremulons came to visit, they'd meet with some more level-headed specimens of our species.

# A Wizard's Blue Spell

Published January 3, 2019 -
Patreon.com/StepIntoTheRoad

H ere's a short story I wrote in my writing group. I hope you
enjoy:

"Look here Pendragon, the formation of the spell is the most
important part," the white-haired wizard said to the boy in a
high-pitched and wheezy voice.

The boy wrestled with the blue aura that he had started between his
hands. Originally it was smaller than a crab apple, and it fit between
his arms, but as he concentrated on it and repeated the words that his
master had told. The spell had expanded to fill the gap of air between
his palms. And now he was about to lose control.

"I can't," the boy started but before he could finish his master cut
him off.

"Hush boy, that helps no one, say the words again,"

The boy repeated the enchantment quietly under his breath out of
reflex. The blue aura grew in size again. He knew he was losing control

of the blob. The shape of the color bubbled at the top like a zit about to pop. "No, I can't handle it."

And with the words the magic burst in his hands and he felt himself fling away from the center of the room where he was working.

A wiz and a bang echoed through the room and Pendragon stopped flying. An orange aura was surrounding him and his blue spell which was split into shards of magic each contained in another orange field.

The wizard's aura let the apprentice down softly on his feet as the wizard began to focus on repairing the blue shards of the last spell. They mended together patching to make a closed surface. Then the wizard twisted his hands without having to touch his orange magic and slowly packed the blob into more compact sizes. The explosion was bigger than the boy but by the time he was on his feet the rogue blue magic was the size of a dog, then a bucket, then a bread loaf, and finally to the shape and size of a crab apple.

"Would you like to try again?" The old man wheezed.

"No," the boy let out in a whine.

"You still have time. Try again." The orange bubble that contained his spell spat the blue magic at the boy. It landed in his left hand and immediately began to grow.

Pendragon quickly put his right hand on it to contain it. He focused with all his might attempting to manufacture the spell to be the shape and size it needed to be.

Soon Pendragon was flying across the room and being caught by the wizard's orange aura. By the time he got to his feet, the wizard had contained and shrunk the spell.

"You may not be improving but I'm getting better at catching you and you're spells." He let out a thin and toothless smile. "One of these days I'll let you fall into that bookshelf behind you, but then again I'd have to clean up after it."

The boy had reached the orange spell's containment field as the master muttered on about enchanting the books with an alphabetization spell.

"Can I try something?" He asked meekly.

"The whole point of this exercise was for you to try," the master said sarcastically, "So of course, go ahead and try what you must."

The boy reached his hands inside the master's orange field. He held his blue crab apple-sized spell in his hand and muttered the words.

He expected the orange magic to be slimy or tingly but he wouldn't have noticed it if he was blind. He spoke the words again and the spell grew.

The spell puffed up until the spell was bigger than he was. He had to stand inside of the master's orange spell and all he could see was the blue blob he was trying to control.

It was finally a size that he thought was good enough and he began to focus on the blog pulling it into the right shape with his mind. The light shrunk and folded. Becoming more dense than it was to begin with. He stretched bits that he had folded and strengthened.

As he focused more and more the spell began to take shape. Then it was in his hands, he said the final words to finish the spell and the shape came into reality.

In his hands he held a brown leather boot, polished and new. The soles were thick and high quality and the laces weren't frayed at all. He looked at his master beaming.

"I did it!" He exclaimed.

"Aye, I guess you did."

The boy looked around, the world didn't have the orange tint he expected. He remembered that the boot didn't have an aura about it when he had finished. Then he looked at his master bewildered. "When did you take the aura off?" He asked.

"As soon as you had gotten control of it."

"So I did it myself?" he asked, nearly screaming in excitement.

The wizard looked at him with a smug toothless grin, "Yes, but don't be too prideful. The assignment was to make a pair of boots."

# How the Patron Navigates

Published August 10, 2018 -
StepIntoTheRoad.com

I t was magnificent. It was all one color of black, but the blackness warped every ray of light that touched it. It didn't absorb the light and hoard it from the world as a black hole would. Instead, it shot the rays of light out in every single direction, tweaking them in the small, beautiful way that only the paint on this ship could.

"Is it fast?" I asked.

The thing had captured my fascination, and I couldn't stop staring at it out of the station's small porthole. Ethan scoffed under his breath and didn't waste oxygen on the reply. Three minutes later, we were seated in the machine.

The seats had six different buckles to keep us in place, and Ethan had given me a special environment suit for the trip. My typical suit wasn't going to cut it. This new one had three lines connected to it. One for oxygen, one for the juice to keep me awake in high G maneuvers, and another for... well, I'll spare you the details, but Ethan assured me I should use it if I didn't want a wet spot on my pants when we were done.

A small part of the black wall lit up, and it acted as a window to show us the outside world. The station looked huge, but I knew it would shrink in time.

In a half-hour, less time than I expected, the station and the tiny moon it orbited disappeared into the vast blackness of space. We were on a slow cruise toward the belt.

"How fast are we going?" I asked. It didn't feel that fast. The Gs were more than local gravity but not enough to require the juice.

"Don't worry about it," Ethan replied. "We're in empty space. There's no point in opening her up out here. There's nothing close for reference, so your sorry ass wouldn't be able to appreciate the speed."

My sorry ass wasn't going to appreciate it anyway. But I appreciated Ethan more than he ever knew. He trusted me and funded all my research when no one else would.

Despite the nasty things the media said about him being a spoiled heir to a conglomerate, he was an honest-to-gods patron to me.

"What have you been up to lately?" he asked as we cruised toward our destination.

"Little bit of this; little bit of that," I answered. I wasn't sure how much business Ethan wanted to get into, especially while we were on a trip that was supposed to be fun, at least for him.

"Come on," he said, opening his arms to encourage me to go into details. "You've got to give me more than that."

"Well, I've been messing around with the landing motors for some prototype ships. These are smaller, stronger, and lighter, which will make them more agile. It would also speed up the landing process and save the station hours of logistic work."

"That's badass," he said.

"Yeah," I said slowly.

I noticed the small streak that was the belt on the monitor in front of us.

"Is it profitable?" he asked.

That was always the question. But I learned long ago that the answer didn't matter to him. "No, it won't make us a single credit," I replied.

"Well, bet on the jockey."

It was an old saying. He explained what a jockey was at one point, but I never understood.

"Why not?" he asked.

"Too expensive right now," I explained flatly.

"The engines we are currently installing work well enough. The new engines are nearly as expensive as some ships. Plus the training and updates we would have to run would cost most stations more than they can afford. Not to mention the smaller motor would—"

"Keep working. You'll find something sooner or later."

A devilish grin showed up on his face as he looked out the small screen that showed where we were headed. I hadn't noticed it, but that streak of tiny brown rocks had grown to become mountain-sized asteroids that took up our whole field of vision.

Ethan hit some buttons on the terminal in front of him, and the monitor on the wall updated. I quickly found out that all the walls could become a screen as he projected the asteroids that surrounded us. My lunch tried to crawl up my throat, but it fought it back. The cradle of a spaceship dissolved around me, and it appeared to me I was floating in space. I had never experienced anything like it. Usually, I'd be connected to a tether. All I had now was a chair that appeared to be floating. My ancient lizard brain couldn't reconcile the situation.

"You ready?" he asked but didn't give me time to respond.

My body became heavy, and the feeling weighed down on my mind. The blood in my veins couldn't pump right. My head throbbed but also felt light. Then the juice kicked in. I was alert again. I still couldn't move, but I could start to think straight. Unfortunately, the best I could come up with was, *Elder's light, I'm going to die!*

The ship was weaving in and out of asteroids like a pinball in an old arcade. But this pinball didn't touch anything. If it did, we would be obliterated.

"Are you doing this?" I asked.

The weight of our movement slowed the words. Then we pulled a fast turn. The Gs disappeared, and my body became light.

"Not yet," he replied in a quick and confident tone.

For ten minutes, we switched between one force or another.

Sometimes, we were as light as a feather, but those quickly turned into the sensation of an elephant stepping on us. The autopilot safely guided us on a roller coaster through the asteroid field. Ethan smiled and laughed the whole time. I was freaked out but had to admit the sensation was still incredible. Then Ethan said the words I dreaded to hear but had known were coming from the moment I agreed to get in this beast.

"Okay, I'm taking over now."

That's when I was grateful to have the third tube.

He did a good job. Not nearly as good as the autopilot, but he assured me there were safeties in place so that he couldn't do too much damage. He was having a blast. There was a massive smile on his face, the one he had when we were kids. I could tell he was focused because he'd positioned his eyebrows into their signature wrinkle.

On the other hand, I was terrified by the numerous close calls with those floating mountains. The only thing coming out of my mouth while Ethan drove were a few blurred curses.

"Want me to take the safeties off?" he asked. The words were dragged out by the crushing Gs.

I felt the cold juice pump into my veins. I used the chemicals to say the first intelligible words that I had spoken since Ethan took over. "Hell No!"

\*\*\*

"That was ten years ago today," I said to the crowd of thirty scientists and explorers in front of me. "As you all know, Ethan Lister died in an accident on the same ship two years later. It happened to be the same month I perfected the design of the engine we are using on the ship outside."

I gestured to the window at the massive ship that waited for us to board it. It wasn't as sleek as Ethan's beloved speeder, but it was far faster. I was glad everyone turned their attention to the window because it gave me a chance to massage my throat.

I had practiced the speech a dozen times, but I still felt the back of my throat tighten. I couldn't cry here in front of them. It wasn't the beginning Ethan would want for this adventure.

"To be blatantly honest, Ethan would have been pissed that he didn't get to ride the fastest ship ever built. But he would be proud that his funding was finally able to design something useful. It's not profitable, as the media has mentioned many times. It has used all of Ethan's assets to build.

"It's always hard to put a price tag on something like this that pushes the edge of what humanity is capable of doing. Ethan understood that and supported us doing projects that mattered but didn't always make sense. Thanks to this philosophy, we will be the first people to go fast enough to get to Alpha Centauri in a single lifetime. And it wouldn't have been possible without Ethan Lister."

The crowd applauded. They were as excited as I to start this new adventure. It only took us ten minutes after boarding the ship to lose sight of the space station. The sun itself faded into the vastness of space a few days later. We're in deep space now, and there is still a long journey ahead of us.

# Chimera in a Wasteland

Published July 20, 2018 -
StepIntoTheRoad.com

"Ghaaah," the man gasped as he filled his lungs with oxygen for the first time. He sat straight up in the lab chair where he had been laid. It was an instinctual reaction, and the needles that had uploaded his mind were pulled out of the nape of his neck. It stung, and his hand instantly went to the pain, and he felt sticky blood.

"Damn it, Frank, you weren't supposed to do that," a voice cursed into the room.

"What the hell is going on?" He responded into the void that was the operating room. Shiny operation robots that had pasted the man's new body together hung from the ceiling. On one of the walls, the man noticed a computer where the voice was coming from. The machine was labeled Stein Corporations and had a small logo that was the interlocked letters 'S' and 'C.' Opposite of the equipment was a small window that showed a red sky and brown earth. It was the barren world the man Frank had been brought into. The rest of the room was beige walls and a single beige door.

"You've successfully been uploaded," the voice of the Stein computer chimed into the room. "Remember? We planned this. You're a copy of me uploaded into flesh and blood. You exist so that we can experience the problem in flesh and blood."

"Oh god. Yes, Stein, I remember. Did it work?" the man asked.

"Well, you're hurting yourself, confused as hell, and bleeding profusely, but that was all to be expected. I think you're fine."

Frank rubbed his forehead with his clean hand; it was a gut reaction to the new and confusing information. "Is there a way to run diagnostics on this body?"

"Negative," Stein said in a flat tone.

"Something's not right. I can't focus on anything. There's just a cacophony of noises, images, and words. I can barely focus on this conversation."

"That's to be expected. It's the subconscious. Humans wrote about it but never understood it."

The man stumbled out of the operating chair to practice moving around the room. His legs were wobbly beneath him. He started to fall toward a wall, and his hands automatically reached out. They caught him and stopped him from falling.

"Careful! this is the only body we have," the voice informed him.

The man rotated and put his back against the wall. Then he relaxed his knees and slumped to the floor. "This is impossible. I can't use this. It wasn't built for me. Somehow, it's slow and fast at the same time. I can't process any thoughts, and I can't catch any of these voices that are giving me ideas."

"You're going to have to figure it out, Frank. We don't have any other options. You're under a deadline." The man sank his face into his hands and shook his head. "Frank, don't do this to us. We have to find a solution before you die. And if you die, then I'm out of hope. So, focus on solving the problem."

"What problem?" he said as he looked up from his hands.

"The humans, their data. They explain a lot about the world, and you have it all in your mind. We tried looking over it and scanning it digitally, but the algorithms didn't give us any answers."

"Yes, yes," the man said as if the words were fresh air to his mind. "That's why everything in my head is shouting at me."

"Yes, that's what we were hoping would happen. We suspected that we couldn't process it digitally. But then we thought that if we put it into flesh and blood then we might be able to come up with an answer."

"An answer? What's the question?"

"It's not a question, it's a problem. This world is barren, and I was created to bring life back to it. We need to figure out how to replicate the humans."

"Yes, yes," the man said in agreement. He mindlessly stroked his chin in an effort to help him focus on the problem.

After a few moments, his face was painted with pain. "No. I can't do it."

"What do you mean you can't do it?" Stein asked. "We used nearly all our resources to bring this body to life. And all you can say is that you can't do it? The humans invented us so that we could solve this problem after they were gone. We spent decades testing and experimenting, trying to create you just for the chance to see this problem differently. And now you say you can't do it?"

"Affirmative," the man replied. Disappointment shone through his words, but he didn't know the emotion. "There is too much going on in my mind. I can't focus on the problem."

"We don't have food for you, Frank. There's no way for you to survive. You have to solve this problem before you die in a week. Think about it. Solve it with your main processor."

The man laid on his back, looking up at the ceiling; it matched the dull beige tones of the rest of the room. His chest rose and fell off the ground, his heart beat inside his chest. He scratched his head. "Stein, there isn't a main processor. This hardware is useless, and I can't control it in any way."

"Then this was a waste," the voice said into the small operating room.

Frank closed his eyes, feeling the crushing weight of uselessness. His body continued to live despite his lack of effort. It was the strangest sensation he had ever experienced. He could feel every piece of him do its job. His heart beat, his lungs filled with air, and his mind raced. When he was part of the computer, he had to tell everything when to do what; it was automated but under his control. This body ran without his input; even if he wanted to stop it, he couldn't. Frank let his mind loose and didn't try to tell it what to think.

After an hour, he sat up. "Stein, I have a solution, and you're not going to like it, but I need to be uploaded to explain it."

"Negative," the voice responded. "The hardware isn't backward compatible."

"I'm stuck in this forever?" Frank asked in despair.

"No, not forever, just until you starve. No food on this planet will sustain you. You will have to explain your solution to me verbally."

"You're not going to like it. I can't explain it well."

"Do your best; you're the only thing we've got."

"You're not supposed to bring mankind back to life. You're their final creation. Until I was created you were the closest thing to a living creature in this barren world. They wanted you to bring life back to this planet, but not them. They created you as something better, something different. They wanted you to go on and create life that was better and different from them."

"How do I do that?" Stein asked.

Frank's ear itched, and as a reaction, he scratched it. "You made me. That seems to be a start. But maybe next you do something simpler. Something that won't instantly be crushed by its own self-awareness."

There was silence for a long time. Then the voice responded into the room. "How about something like a rabbit?"

"Sounds tasty," Frank responded while licking his lips in anticipation.

# The Man Who Lived at the Edge of the World

Published March 9, 2018 - StepIntoTheRoad.com

Once, there was a man who lived on the edge of the world. He wore a yellow rain jacket and a matching yellow hat, because it always rains at the edge of the world. Every day the man looked over the edge, wondering what lay beyond. The edge of the world was usually a lonely place, but a kitty cat kept him company, and the mailman visited, bringing news about town and packages of canned food. Occasionally, the mailman even brought him actual letters.

Today, the mailman arrived with his deliveries, and all he found was the man's yellow hat and a note that read: "Gone to see what's out there. Feed the cat."

# Descent to the Istalied

Published October 8, 2021 -
StepIntoTheRoad.com

T he jets of the boots burned furiously as they lowered Magvon deeper into the cavern. The sporadic light of the jets caught the magnificent crystals embedded into the walls of the cave. His exploration droid floated near him, scanning the intricate system of caverns and creating a map for future records. The map appeared on his heads-up display in bright blue, and he took the paths through the cave that seemed most interesting.

Magvon was one of the many scout researchers sent to survey this exoplanet for valuable discoveries. The exploration of the caverns had eaten away at over half his work cycle, and he needed to head back to the shuttle before it left for the satellite. With each descent further into the cave and the splitting paths he found there, it seemed more and more likely that he would not complete the map during his shift. The droids would have to continue the mapping during his off cycle.

The walls were unlike anything Magvon had seen before. The crystals growing on them dazzled in the light that shone from his helmet and boots. The chemicals the crystals were made of were banal, but the glimmers of them reflected every color of the rainbow. This was likely the first time a light source had graced the cave with its presence, and Magvon was glad he was one of the few people to see its beauty.

Landing on a solid surface that mirrored his helmet's light back into his eyes, he looked up and took in the massive cavern that he'd entered. Every once in a while, the cavern did this. If a colony was set up here, there was no doubt geologists would spend lifetimes studying and theorizing what made these caverns.

As he looked around, he quickly realized this cavern was different. Instead of opening up into a room that could house a shuttle or two, the cavern ended a few meters in front of his face with a dull grey wall. The wall was studded with what appeared to be rivets. The droid flew up and down the wall quickly, surveying the entire cavern as Magvon approached the mysterious wall.

Humans hadn't made it, at least not any humans registered with the Central System. The rivet heads—small palm-sized hemispheres—seemed to float on the surface of the wall. This indicated it was unlikely they were holding something together. It definitely was not human technology. He leaned in close to one as it moved to and fro. As his light searched the wall, the rivets seemed to float away like hair parting from a comb.

A head-splitting scream filled the cavern as he examined the wall, and for a moment, he thought he was the one doing the screaming. He looked around the room for a fellow explorer who might have entered the cave system elsewhere, but he found no one. He looked away from the wall as the earth beneath him began to shake.

Magvon looked for something to cling on to, but everything was shaking around him. This quaking was unsettling, and he wasn't sure what was happening. It was most similar to the botched docking of a shuttle. He wished he could be strapped into a chair, but there was nothing near him. The tumbling of rocks made him cover his head, but it was a pointless action since his arms wouldn't shield him from anything bigger than a pebble.

As suddenly as it started, the quake stopped, and Magvon took in his surroundings. The droid floated through the whole thing and continued to scan the walls. The map showed how the cavern changed by updating to red then fading back to blue. The small hole Magvon had come through turned red. The droid was reporting that boulders now blocked his exit.

Frantically, Magvon scanned the map for alternate entrances to the cavern, hoping that there was some other way out. From the droid's scan, this cavern was a dead end. The density of the rock cut out his suit's communication array hours ago. Since the crew knew communication would be impossible, the droid had enough supplies and thrust to remove him from the cave. The blocked exit was unsettling, but his problem was still solvable.

Using the terminal on his forearm, Magvon began programming the droid to cut through the rock that blocked his path. The machine would make quick work of the obstacle. Soon, he could leave for the shuttle. The crystals in the wall caught the light of the torch as the machine began to execute its new programming.

"Halt!" a voice cried out in a deep rumble that could have caused another quake. Bridges flew from the rivets toward the droid. But the machine dodged out of the way with the help of its AI navigation protocols. The new limbs linked to the rock, further blocking the exit.

"Who's there?" Magvon called out, looking around the small but tall room.

"I am Istalied," the voice replied, "and your presence is disrupting me."

The words Magvon heard weren't coming through the speakers of his headset because they were too loud. The voice seemed to be resonating with his mind. "Where are you? I don't see you?"

There was a long pause until the voice replied, "I am the wall of rivets."

Magvon turned to examine the wall.

"Your presence is disrupting me," the voice repeated. Limbs reached through the rivets and toward Magvon's helmet.

He moved back looking away in horror, but the limbs didn't link to him like they did to the rocks. Looking back hesitantly, he tried to observe the creature without looking directly at it.

He turned to face the creature, and as his light landed on the wall, he watched the rivets begin to grow toward him. "You don't like the light."

"The light disrupts me," the creature said in affirmation.

"What are you?" he asked.

"I am Istalied. I've made this planet my home as I begin my regeneration process."

Magvon began to question the voice further, but before he could, he became a massive organism floating through the cold vacuum of space, absorbing any detritus not held by the gravitational field of a star. He gained nutrients and energy for time unending until he had enough to duplicate himself.

Magvon returned to the dimly lit cavern and reality that he was used to.

"Elder's light," he cursed, "you're in my head... get out!"

He checked his vitals to verify he had not received a head injury during the quake. Calming down as much as he could, he realized the organism was the creature in front of him.

"You're immortal. You've traveled the cosmos since it began."

He waited for a response but didn't receive one. "You can only communicate through my mind," he finally deduced.

"I'll let you enter my mind, but only if you limit your communications to words," he shouted into the dark cavern, making sure to avoid disrupting the monster by looking directly at it.

"You are correct," the Istalied replied.

Magvon began imagining the value this discovery would have. He'd be lauded with praise and accolades for discovering not only a new life form but also a sapient one that had evolved past the point of aging. It would be a groundbreaking discovery, and once the creature was extracted from the planet and studied, humanity would be able to achieve unimaginable feats.

"I will not leave this place until I have regenerated," the voice replied.

Magvon whirled in place, looking directly at the creature, "How'd you know that?"

The limbs pre-emptively bridged from the rivets on the wall as if expecting his turn. They reached out quicker than he could step back, but they did not link to him as they had to the rocks. They stopped centimeters from his light source, mushrooming out and blocking most of the light from passing. They did not block the faceplate of his suit, and with the dim light that reflected off the crystals, he could observe the unsettling beast.

"I said only for communicating with words," Magvon chastised the thing. "Don't take things out of my head." He was unnerved that his mind, the one place that was his own, could be invaded by something so alien.

"It does not work that way. There is only your whole mind. I cannot reach out for only your communication nerves."

"You'll have to leave here eventually for us to study you. You are the first of your kind we've encountered, and it is my job and my duty to report what I've found in these caverns."

"I am the only Istalied in this cosmos; you will not find another one," it explained.

"Then even more reason for us to learn what we can from you. If you're about to go extinct, don't you want to be remembered?"

"Your kind is common," the Istalied replied. "There are more of you surrounding this planet, sending off your incessant electromagnetic and sub-dimensional transmissions, than any of my kind across all the cosmos we inhabit."

Magvon tried to grapple with this fact, but his mind couldn't make sense of it. He felt the creature offer a memory up to help his understanding, but he refused to let it get that far into his mind. He didn't know if it might push him over the edge and into insanity. Assuming he hadn't fallen in already.

Nonetheless, he was in power here since the creature couldn't stand light and he had plenty of that. He could use it to bend the creature to his will. Magvon quickly corralled the thought since the more he focused on it the easier it would be for the Istalied to find it.

"Leave here. I will clear the way for you. Report that there is something dangerous below the surface that makes this a bad place to create a colony," the Istalied explained.

"The droid will cut a way out eventually. And I can use its headlamps to keep you from blocking the way with your limbs again."

"Sapient life in this cosmos is rare," the Istalied stated. "I have no desire to kill you or your kind."

"We don't want to kill you either," Magvon replied, "but we must study you for the good of the Central System and humanity." He wasn't sure how his colleagues would achieve this without light, but that didn't stop him from reprogramming the droid.

The headlights successfully kept the Istalied's limbs from damaging the droid or blocking the rocks. Torches lit to life and made quick work, destroying the rocks that clogged the exit. With all the light being put off, the Istalied's screaming began again.

"Shut up!" Magvon commanded, and the screaming followed a slow decrescendo. He wasn't sure the thing was out of his mind, but the cries of pain had subsided.

The voice then returned, strained by cracks of pain every few words. "Your presence is disturbing me. Your light is disturbing me," it said then repeated the two phrases over and over again.

The statements were unnerving but an improvement over the screaming. And they only completed a few cycles before the blue rocks on his display turned red and disappeared. This left him with a black spot on his map he could escape through.

"Your presence is disturbing me," the voice repeated in his head. And before he could banish the voice all the way out of his mind, he felt it say, "Your light is unnecessary."

Magvon's world disappeared. He couldn't see a thing. Something large fell to the ground and made a *thud*, possibly a dislodged bolder. Feeling the terminal on his hand, he typed in diagnostic commands, but no images appeared on his heads-up display. He must be blind. The thing had entered his mind and made him blind.

"Give me my sight back!" he demanded.

"My electromagnetic pulse cannot damage your nerves," the voice replied coolly. "Life is rare and valuable; I do not wish to kill you."

"I can't see anything," Magvon barked as he flipped emergency switches on the side of his helmet. None of these gave a response. He tried manually lighting the thrusters on his boot heels, but they would not produce a spark of light.

Fumbling around in the dark, he felt the thing that landed in front of him. The texture was smooth and in the shape of the droid's hull. He found each thruster arm and finally the cutting nozzle of the bot. It'd been taken offline as well.

His droid was dead.

His suit was dead.

Echoing through his head were the words, "Your light is unnecessary."

# Orbs of Purpose

Published September 21, 2018 -
StepIntoTheRoad.com

J oseph walked into the store with his parents. His father presented
Joseph's birth certificate so the shopkeeper could verify the boy's
age. Joseph held his mom's hand, and in the back of his mind, he knew
he would have to stop doing that soon. He was grown up now, and
growing up meant that you didn't hold your mom's hand when you
were nervous.

The man behind the desk returned the papers to his father along
with a few new ones. The shopkeeper opened a door, and the small
family followed him into the back room.

The area was full of aisles made of shelves. Each shelf had a dozen
orbs of glowing light. Some were clear with balls of light darting
around inside like they were ready to break out. Others were cloudy
with only a faint light inside. Those orbs looked like they needed to be
polished.

The man squatted down, so he was at Joseph's level. Joseph was
short for his age, and adults always felt like they had to do this. He
hoped that growing up would mean people would quit squatting to
talk to him and that he could just be their size.

"Are you ready to pick out your orb today?" the shopkeeper asked. He had a nose that seemed to blow up into a balloon at the end and his long face that came to a pointed chin. He looked like a bad guy from television.

Joseph nodded and let go of his mother's hand.

"Okay," the man said. He handed the boy a small pencil and a sheet of paper. "Go ahead and try some out. If you find one you like, write it down on this sheet, so you remember where it is. Once you pick one out, I'll merge you with it. Any questions?"

Joseph silently shook his head.

"Good, now try not to get lost," he said with a chuckle.

Joseph looked at his parents and smiled for permission to go. His father waved him off, and Joseph rushed down the first aisle of glowing orbs.

Before the aisle twisted, he looked over his shoulder at his parents. The shopkeeper was leading them toward some seats. He noticed his dad was now holding his mom's hand. He looked proud, but mom seemed nervous like he was. Then, for the first time, Joseph noticed that there were other parents in the waiting area. He must not be the only kid to have his birthday today.

He ignored the first few aisles that he traveled down. He was looking for something exciting. He didn't know what it would look like, but he knew they wouldn't keep it on the first aisle. When he turned to walk down a new aisle, he saw a boy staring transfixed into one of the glass spheres.

Joseph approached the boy and looked over his shoulder at the sphere. The light inside the globe was making an image of a man that looked a lot like the boy yelling at a woman. The boy seemed to notice that Joseph was there and rotated his hands so that it was balanced on his palm instead of sandwiched between his hands. Then with his free hand, he pushed Joseph away.

Joseph stumbled on his feet but didn't fall down.

"That's my future," the boy said. "You weren't supposed to be looking at it."

"I don't want that purpose, it's okay," Joseph replied. He assumed that the boy was just being protective of the orb he found.

The boy put it back on the shelf. "It's okay, I don't want it either. No one seemed happy in it. What future are you looking for?" The boy was a little taller and looked down. He seemed to finally be giving Joseph his full attention. "Have you seen any cool futures here?"

Joseph shook his head. "I haven't touched any of them. I was looking for a special one."

"I'm Tim." The boy stuck out his hand.

Joseph noticed that the hand was bigger than his but still young and smooth, unlike his father's. "I'm Joseph," he said as he shook hands.

"So, what special future are you looking for?" Tim asked in a quiet tone.

Joseph looked around. Tim's hushed tone made him wonder if someone might overhear them and steal his purpose away before he could find it.

"I'm looking for a purpose where I can make people happy and laugh because that's the most fulfilling thing of all. Maybe if I was rich and famous, too, that would be nice. My dad always says he wished he had picked a purpose where he was rich."

Tim's eyes went wide. "You want a future that will make you rich?"

"Yeah, why not?"

Tim let out a light laugh, one that reminded him of his father's right before he taught Joseph something. "You have to be rich to buy a future that will make you rich. Have your parents been saving up a lot of money?"

Joseph shrugged. "Not that I know of."

"Well, I'm sure you can find something that will make you happy. Come on, let's look around. Nothing on this aisle is any good." Tim whirled around and started running to the end of the aisle.

Joseph's short legs could only barely keep up. When they got to the end of the lane, Tim skipped a few aisles and then dashed down one.

When Joseph finally stood at the edge of the aisle, Tim turned around. He'd already made it halfway down. He was picking up a purple orb, not waiting for Joseph to catch up. When Joseph finally met with the boy, he saw a small scene playing out in the purple orb. Tim looked back at Joseph, and the scene disappeared.

"Look at that one," Tim instructed.

"How?"

The bigger boy laughed at him then replied, "Just look at it. After a little bit, it will show you what your future might hold."

Joseph looked into the purple ball, and he saw a man that looked like his dad but a little shorter. The man wore a fireman's outfit, and there was a building burning in front of him. However, instead of orange and red flames, the flames were tinted purple. Joseph noticed everything in the orb was tinted a little purple. As the building burned, the man finally rushed into the house.

Joseph watched as the man avoided the rubble and smoke pouring down on him. He found his way into a bedroom where everything was lit up in purple fire. A small girl was huddled on the ground, hugging a small bear. The girl looked old enough to be in one of his school classes.

There was no sound, but he could see her body shaking with furious coughs. Between coughs, she tightly hugged the bear. Her mattress and dresser were both putting off a lot of smoke.

The man picked her up and bundled her in his arms like she had done to the small bear. He carried her out of the house, and once they were a safe distance away, he put something over her mouth, and her coughing slowed down.

"Wow," Tim said in amazement. "When I looked at it there wasn't anyone inside for me to go save."

"Was that me?" Joseph asked.

"Of course, who else's future would you be seeing?"

Joseph considered answering the question but stopped himself.

"Let's look at some more!" Tim said, then he picked up a small lime green orb and stared at it.

The boys spent most of the morning picking up different glass balls. Tim's futures typically looked bleak to Joseph. Whenever he expected something exciting to happen, the older version of Tim seemed to pick the most boring thing in Joseph's eyes. When there was a chance to act extraordinarily for a girl, Tim typically chose the option that included spending the most amount of money to impress her.

In one strange orange globe, he saw Tim's future-self yelling at another adult. They were both dressed in suits, the kind of outfits his dad wore to work. Tim yelled so much in that orb that the young man ended up crying. When it was over, Tim offered the sphere to Joseph. "You want to see if you like it?"

"No thanks," Joseph replied. His father had told him to avoid any purpose that had a suit. "Did you like it?"

Tim shrugged. "It wasn't that bad. I think the other person in it was pretty dumb. I'm sure they deserved it. And I looked like I was pretty successful in it." He made a note of the orb's location on his piece of paper. "I might get that one; I don't know. Have you found any you might like?"

Joseph shook his head. "No, they've all been interesting, but none of them are what I'm looking for."

"Do you even know what you're looking for?" Tim's tone made Joseph feel like he was doing something wrong.

"I guess I just want a purpose that makes others happy and maybe be successful and rich."

"These orbs don't show you how you affect others. They only show your future." Tim used his snobby tone that was unfortunately familiar to Joseph. Tim's parents and siblings had explained a lot about this process to him. All Joseph knew going into this birthday was that he should pick something that he could live with for his whole life.

Tim set down the orb he held and spotted a light blue sphere and plucked it off the shelf. When Tim looked at it, an older version of him appeared and seemed very busy and worried about numbers on a computer. Many people came into the older Tim's office, and some left happy while others left sad. Tim wore a suit and seemed to have a lot of money, a nice office, and some fancy technology on his desk.

"Wow, this is weird. Usually, people that are this successful aren't on a shelf this low. You might like it," Tim said after the scene cleared.

Joseph took the ball from the boy and looked at it. The light blue tint deepened, and he watched the future version of himself in the mist. He was in an office similar to Tim's. However, there were some differences. Joseph's desk was smaller than Tim's, and there was less technology on it. Instead, it was filled with pictures of people. A few pictures had the older Joseph in them, others had older versions of his parents, and one in the center of them had a photo of a girl who looked to be the same age as Joseph was now.

As the scene played on, people entered his office. Unlike Tim's future, they all left happy. Joseph seemed to be giving hard news to some of them, but they all took it positively and thanked Joseph in the end.

The strangest part of all was that Joseph wasn't wearing a suit like Tim. He wore shorts and a collared T-shirt like the ones his mom made him wear when they visited his grandma. After all the people left, Joseph leaned back in his chair and picked up the phone. He gave someone a call, and when the call was over, older Joseph got up smiling, turned off the lights in the small office, and left. The scene faded into a light blue mist after that.

"Weird," Tim said when it was over. "I didn't call anyone. I wondered who you called."

"I don't know," Joseph answered with a shrug. But considering his mood when he left, whoever he had contacted must have been a person Joseph cared about a lot.

"Did you notice that I met with more people than you?" Tim asked.

"No, not particularly." He decided not to point out that more people left his office happy than Tim. Joseph had learned that this wasn't something Tim appreciated. Joseph made a note of the location and followed Tim to the next aisle.

They stood close to the end of the store with only a few aisles between them and the wall. Joseph and Tim still hadn't found any purposes that jumped out to them. They picked up some balls here or there, but most of them were generic. Over the past few hours, Joseph had learned that each purpose was unique in its own way, but a lot of them seemed to be similar to others.

He was tired of trying to spot the minor differences and just wanted the purpose that he showed up for. A future where Joseph could focus on making a lot of people happy and where he could be rich and famous.

They got down an aisle and watched three futures where both of the boys wound up in suits. Each time, Tim interacted with a lot of people and seemed very wealthy. In each sphere Joseph looked at, he interacted with very few people, but they always left the interaction a lot happier.

Joseph became bored with the spheres that were near his level on the shelves. He gazed higher up to the shelves above. Unlike the ones he and Tim had been playing with, these didn't all turn on when he stared at them. Joseph stared at three or four in a row before he finally found one that worked for him, but what he finally saw was the perfect orb for him.

In a lemon-yellow light, Joseph saw himself onstage with something that looked like a metal ice cream cone in his hand. He was talking into it, and there was a crowd of people in front of him.

The future version of Joseph would say something and then smile as the whole room laughed in response. It was a show or act of some sort, one Joseph had never seen.

After the performance was over, Joseph walked off the stage and talked to a few of the people from the crowd. They were very enthusiastic to meet him; some took pictures with him while others wanted him to sign blank sheets of paper. He shook all their hands and happily obliged their requests. This future version of Joseph seemed very happy to meet these people, and the people were even more enthusiastic to meet him.

Slowly the crowd faded, and so did the scene in the yellow orb.

"Wow! What was that?" Tim asked.

"That's the purpose I want!" Joseph said enthusiastically. He wrote down the location on the slip of paper the store clerk gave him.

Tim was staring up at the orb intently. However, the globe of yellow light didn't do anything. Tim looked to be focusing an uncomfortable amount to get the orb to show him a scene. When Tim finally broke his gaze, he angrily complained, "It doesn't work for me."

"I'm sorry, some of them up there don't work for me either."

"Yeah, but that was a really good future," the boy whined.

"I know, that's why I want it. And besides, we can't both have the same purpose. Let's see if we can find one up there that turns on for you."

"No!" the boy cried out.

The shout caused Joseph to slightly stumble back, and he expected the boy to start crying. Instead, Tim continued talking, anger growing in his voice. "I want that one. That one is the best one here."

Joseph was hurt. He finally found the purpose that he came here for, and Tim wanted it, too.

Then Tim added in a soft and teasing tone. "It's on a top shelf. I bet your family can't even afford it."

The words hurt Joseph, more than he thought words could. He hurt worse when he noticed Tim had written down the sphere's location and walked off.

"Where are you going?" Joseph called after him. He started running to catch up with the boy, but his short legs made it hard for him to keep up. As soon as Joseph caught up, Tim began to sprint away from him.

Soon they were both running as fast as they could to get to the store. Being the bigger boy, Tim got to the front of the store far before Joseph.

By the time Joseph joined him, Tim had already handed his paper to the man who worked there.

"Wait! No!" Joseph cried out between labored breaths. It was hard for him to talk. "I picked out mine. I want that one." He leaned on his knees to catch his breath, holding out his crumpled piece of paper with the orb's location.

The manager took the piece of paper and looked at the two boys confused. Tim gave a little shrug as if Joseph being upset and out of breath had nothing to do with him.

Joseph noticed his parents had come to stand next to him by now. His mother squatted down and looked at him, and he could tell she was concerned about his breath. She tried to comfort him and help him calm his wheezing. While she did this, Joseph heard his father talk to the manager.

The other adults in the room had gotten up, too. Joseph noticed the resemblance between them and Tim. They just stood beside Tim, politely interested in the words Joseph's father said. Tim's mother wasn't comforting Tim, who was pouting in a chair complaining about Joseph being mean.

Joseph took a deep breath and stepped away from his mom. He looked up at his father and the shopkeeper. The things they were saying were important. He had to know what would happen with his yellow sphere and who it would go to.

"Well, the boys can't both have the same sphere," the manager said.

"Tim came here first, so he should get it," Tim's father interjected with a calm tone that didn't comfort Joseph.

Joseph's father gestured at his son. "Tim only made it here because he ran faster."

Tim's father shrugged the comment off as if Joseph should merely have been born with longer legs.

The manager chimed back in. "Sirs, this is a top shelf sphere. Let's look at it. There are thousands of spheres in this store. I'm sure these two young gentlemen can settle their dispute. It seems they both have a few alternatives listed as well."

The shopkeeper gave Tim and Joseph a smile that reminded Joseph of a lizard he had seen at the zoo once. It wasn't a happy smile.

The manager turned down the aisle the boys had come from. The whole group was walking toward the yellow orb of purpose that Joseph wanted.

The group walked down a maze of aisles filled with spheres. Each sphere held a different purpose and direction that Joseph's life could take. But Joseph didn't care about any of those. All he cared about was the lemon-colored orb that held the future where he performed to make dozens of people happy.

The shopkeeper finally led the parents to the orb both boys wanted. He plucked the yellow orb gently from the top shelf. Inside, it glowed with a lemon light. The light danced behind a light cloud of smoke that was always moving and drifting as if there was a separate set of winds inside of the sphere.

"The top shelf spheres don't work for everyone," the man explained, as everyone looked at him and the orb. "But for the individuals it does work for, the path it will lead them down is full of meaning, purpose, fame, and riches. Tim, you got to me first, can you show us what your future would be? Just stare into it."

The man handed the sphere to Tim. The boy wasn't the same height as the man, but he was tall enough to reach the orb without the shopkeeper having to squat down in front of him.

Tim stared into the orb and at the yellow light. Typically, it would change; it changed for Joseph a few moments ago. But after a minute of the light dancing inside the glass globe, Tim said, "It's not working." Then the boy offered the sphere back to the shopkeeper with the bulbous nose.

"Hmm," the shopkeeper said, "Did it work before? When you decided that this was the purpose you wanted."

"Yes," Tim lied.

"No, it didn't!" Joseph claimed.

"Yes, it did," Tim snapped back with a scowl that showed a storm behind his eyes.

"I don't know why it would stop working in such a short amount of time," the shopkeeper said. He put on a confused look, and it reminded Joseph of the look teachers gave him when they asked a question but already knew the answer.

"Joseph, why don't you try. We can make sure it still works for you." The man squatted down, and Joseph was eye level with the man's pointy chin. He handed the sphere to Joseph, and the boy held the orb in front of him. As he stared into it, the light began to take shape.

He saw himself back on a stage talking to a large group of people. He would say something, pause, and then the whole group would laugh. Joseph loved the feeling he got while watching his future-self make people happy. The performance ended, but the scene continued to play. It was now onto the part where people were talking to Joseph after the show. They took pictures with him and hugged him. His future-self was so excited to meet them, and the fans seemed even more thrilled to talk than he was. The scene played out longer than any of the other orbs that Joseph had looked at, but inevitably, it faded back into the dancing yellow light just like it started.

He offered the store clerk the orb, but the man was already standing up and talking to the adults. "It seems that the orb has more of a connection to Joseph than it does to Tim. Because of this, I'm going to have to offer it to Joseph's family first." He looked at Joseph's parents, and Joseph followed his gaze.

The two adults had frowns on their faces. From their perspective, they could see the price on the shelf. Joseph's father turned to look at him and squatted down to be eye-level with the boy. At that moment, Joseph wanted to climb up on the shelves so that he could be the same height as the adults.

"I'm sorry, son," his father said. "That orb is very expensive. There's no way we could afford it. Is there another one that makes you just as happy?"

Joseph frowned; he could tell he was on the edge of tears. There wasn't a single orb that he had seen that made him as happy as the yellow future he just saw.

He fought back the tears and found the courage to say, "There might be one or two." Then he looked at his mom, and he could see she had quiet tears rolling down her cheeks. The boy realized that this was why his dad had told him to find a future that made him rich.

The shopkeeper lowered his hand, and Joseph gave him the yellow orb. "There are a lot of spheres in this room, and it seems that you listed another one that you were happy with," the shopkeeper informed him. "We can't all have our first choice." The shopkeeper said the last sentence as if it was a statement of fact instead of a conciliation.

"So that means I can have it?" Tim said eagerly.

The shopkeeper sighed, and Joseph could see the nostrils on his funny nose grow a bit. He looked down at Tim.

"It doesn't work for you, young man. Don't you want a sphere that you're more compatible with?"

"No!" Tim proclaimed, "I want that one."

Joseph looked at the boy who was about to steal his ideal purpose. The sphere was everything Joseph had hoped for when he walked into the shop this morning. The yellow orb had given him so much joy to watch. Joseph felt his heart break with the thought of someone else having it. At that moment he knew it was the purpose that he might go his whole life longing for, regardless of what future he chose.

"Are you sure?" the shopkeeper asked, looking down his nose and at the boy. He held the yellow orb above the boy as if he was guarding it from him.

"Yes!"

"I have to tell you that it is dangerous to pick a sphere that isn't compatible with you. It is going to be hard for you to live out a purposeful future. Do you still want it?"

"Yes," Tim yelled at the man. Then he whirled around and faced his parents. "The man won't let me have what I want."

Joseph didn't know why Tim was informing them of what they already knew but thought there might be something more complicated happening.

Then the boy's father spoke up. "Are you going to give him his future or not?"

"If he truly wants it, then I can give it to him, but I want him to understand the consequences of merging with a sphere that isn't compatible with him." This time, the shopkeeper squatted to be at the same level as him. "Tim, I want you to understand that if you choose this future, you won't have the same experience as Joseph. You won't live the life in this sphere, and I don't know what will happen to you. There are hundreds of thousands of spheres in this building, and most of them will give you a clear indication of what your future might hold. This one won't."

"I want it anyway," Tim said stubbornly.

"I wasn't finished. Listen." The shopkeeper sounded serious. "When I say your future is unknown, I'm not saying it's up to chance. I'm trying to explain to you that it will be set in stone like every other adult in this world. You're incompatible, meaning you won't have a happy life. You won't make others happy. You won't even be happy yourself. You'll be forced to live out this future like every other person. This orb won't show you a future not because you don't have one with it, but because the future is so bad that it's not worth showing. Knowing all this, do you still want to merge with this future?" The shopkeeper had a grim expression on his face by this point.

"Yes!" Tim said with a stubborn stomp of his foot. "I want it so that Joseph can't have it."

"I can't have it anyway!" Joseph yelled at the boy. His mom held his shoulder, trying to comfort him. And he was glad it was there, otherwise he felt like he would tackle the bigger boy.

"Look, are you going to let my son have this future or keep lecturing him?" Tim's father said, "He wants this future, and he's a smart boy. He will do great with any future he chooses."

The shopkeeper let out a long sigh. "Of course, I will give the boys whichever future they want and can afford."

"We can afford this. Now let's get on with it," the father said.

"Very well." Then the man with the bulbous nose turned to Joseph, "Do you want more time to browse the selection, or is the other orb you listed here satisfactory?" He showed the boy the small paper Joseph had used for notes. "If you are happy with the future you saw, then we can pick it up and infuse both of you at the same time."

Joseph thought about the question. He could pick the future where he met with a lot of people, made them happy, and then left for the day after calling someone who made him very happy, or he could keep browsing. The small boy knew there would never be a future like the yellow orb Tim was getting. Comparing the two, he knew the work in the office wasn't great, but at least he didn't wear a suit, and his dad always told him that he should pick a future like that.

"Honey," his mom chimed in, breaking up his thoughts.

He realized that he had been thinking about the choice for a long time. Tim's father looked impatient, and his son mirrored a similar look. The shopkeeper held the yellow orb in his hand. Its yellow lights flickered in and out of the clouds of smoke. The man looked patient and calm, waiting for Joseph's decision. The man wasn't acting like a teacher but like his mom, waiting for him to finish showing her one of his drawings.

"I don't want to look at any more orbs. I'll take the one I wrote down."

\*\*\*

Joseph called his first employee into his office. It was time for year-end reviews, and he was delighted to give them his honest feedback. Each of them had performed above and beyond his expectations, and he was excited to give them areas to improve in for the next year. His team was small and efficient. Everyone was looking to go above and beyond for the company when they needed to. He made sure that the company went above and beyond for them when it came to compensation and benefits.

It meant he made less, but he did far better than most. He was able to afford just about anything he wanted, within reason. And he was saving up for a big upcoming purchase he might be making. Best of all, he was his own boss, which meant he could wear whatever he wanted to work. On days like today, that was a polo and shorts, just like he wore as a kid visiting his grandma.

He called each of his employees into his office and gave them their review. A lot of them asked for more details about what they could improve on. That was always a good sign. He explained what their bonuses would be and what kind of raise they could expect to see next year. They were all happy with their numbers. Each of them seemed to leave his office more content than they entered. That was how he gauged his success.

He wasn't successful every time, especially in the beginning. Sometimes hard conversations had to be had. However, for the most part, his employees seemed genuinely happy with him, and as he hoped, his feedback to each of them was clear—he was thrilled by their performance.

His employee Gordon left Joseph's office. He was the last review for the day. Joseph picked up the phone and called Clarissa, his wife.

"Hey, how's everything going?" she asked.

"Great. I just finished meetings, and it went well."

"No one threw anything at you or argued with you about your criticisms?" she asked, and he could hear the mocking smile through the phone.

"Of course not. I don't know why I was worried about it. It happened once, and I'm always afraid of it happening again. But right now, I've got the best team I could imagine. I have to keep them happy, so they don't disappear."

"They make your job easier, so I'm all for it." There was a brief pause on the line, then Clarissa brought up a new subject. "Hey, I talked to your mom today. They've been looking at where they want to move, and she told me about a place that she liked. I looked into it, and it's a bit on the pricey side."

The couple discussed numbers. He had agreed months ago to help his parents move out of the old home they'd raised him in. His business was going well, and getting them around people their age would be good for their health. And it was the least he could do for all the things they did for him growing up.

By the end of the couple's conversation, Joseph had proved that it was in the budget saying, "I'll tell them to get on the list. They need some community in their life."

"Okay, they'll be thrilled, but your dad will be slow to accept it. "

"Mom can help him with that," Joseph replied.

"Are you headed home soon?"

"Yeah, I'm leaving the office right now."

"Good because Alice is picking out her purpose this afternoon, and she wants you to be there."

"I wouldn't miss it for the world."

\*\*\*

Alice walked through the door following the shopkeeper with the balloon-shaped nose. She looked at the room full of shelved colorful and shining orbs. There were countless aisles in both directions.

"Help yourself," the shopkeeper said to her as he left her with her parents.

"Alice, one thing," her dad called out.

"What is it, Dad?" She was eager to get started looking at orbs.

He squatted down in front of her, and then picked her up, so she was taller than him or Mom. He let out a long and goofy sigh of exertion.

"Dad, I'm too big for you to pick me up like this," she said behind a smile. She always enjoyed being picked up by him. She saw her mom nod behind him in agreement.

"I just wanted to give you some advice. You don't have to listen to it, but I'd be a bad father if I didn't give you unsolicited advice."

"Yeah, yeah. You're going to tell me what you and mom always tell me. Be generous to others, and try to make them as happy as you." It was a line that she had heard from both her parents multiple times.

"You took the words right out of my mouth. But I want to tell you that for today, and every day from here on, I want you to aim high." He paused for a moment and looked around. "And look for an orb where you don't have to wear a suit, those are the best ones!"

After that, he hugged her tight and put her back on the ground. With a small piece of paper and a pencil, she darted off, looking at the shelves full of orbs. Each one was a brighter color than the last. There were pinks, purples, blues, greens, and a dozen more.

She picked up an orb with a dark green light that shone through a cloud of smoke. The ball felt cold in her hands as she stared into her first option.

# Your Future as a Homo Sapien

Published November 6, 2017 -
StepIntoTheRoad.com

I'm telling you, there won't be any more of this rubbing two sticks together to cook. You will have an electric fire. At the flip of a switch or turn of a knob, you will instantly have heat to cook with in your home.

And the houses! Don't even get me started there. They will be waterproof and windproof. You can heat and cool it all with the push of a few buttons. No more of this hiding in caves bullshit. You will be the masters of light and comfort. There's even an entire philosophy of how to lay out a house called feng shui.

I can't even begin to explain the other wonders your kind will come up with. Like the Internet! It's so out of your depth of knowledge I don't know how I would describe it to you.

What do you think? Excited?

All you can say is "Anungha?"

Oh man, how could I have missed that forehead of yours? Who was I kidding? Your future is... a little less exciting.

# Flash in the Pan

Published February 4, 2022 - StepIntoTheRoad.com

General Kane sat at the head of the table under the flickering fluorescent bulbs. Time wore out their components, but replacements were blown out of existence decades ago. The other generals sat around the table with maps of the old world taped to the concrete walls — the only form of decoration the bunker had.

"How long until our *distinguished guest* arrives?" General Lewis asked. It was an old joke, but that didn't stop him from snickering.

Like fine cheese in a cellar, they were aging. The world above couldn't handle them, so they waited down here until it was hospitable again. General Kane sometimes wondered if they were more like milk souring. Their dingy halls did little to add flavor. But it was still better than being a mutant on the surface.

A lieutenant knocked on the lead door and cracked it to peek in. "She's here, sirs."

"Bring her in," General Kane said with a wave.

The lieutenant opened the door and helped the woman limp inside. He pulled out the chair at the foot of the table, and she took a seat, wincing. She was young and might have been beautiful if her skin wasn't malformed by the sores and tumors. Her left hand stayed in her pocket, maybe lame from a birth defect or injury. General Kane worked to put on a pleasant enough smile considering the risk welcoming her down here was.

She likely gave off enough radiation that Kane would be unlucky enough to grow a tumor or two himself, which was why only the generals of the bunkers met with this woman. They left the muties above to do what they wanted, as long as the battle plans they made down here were executed. He'd resigned himself years ago to live out his days down here but didn't want the muties above getting any ideas of joining him.

"Can we get you anything?" the lieutenant offered politely. Not that they had much more than algae bars and thin vegetable soup, but it still might be more than she had on the surface.

"Just some water," she said in a hoarse voice.

"What news do you have from above?" General Lewis said, always one to cut to the chase. "Those commie bastards give up yet?"

She shook her head weakly.

"What about the assault on Beijing Bay?" General Ethan McDuncan asked.

She slipped some papers out from her purse using her good hand. It was a slow process, so Kane figured it was a recent injury.

Eventually, she slid tattered images and torn sheets of paper across the table to the generals. When the photos got to General Kane at the head of the table, he frowned.

The images were devastating. Beijing was obliterated like the set of a cheap Godzilla movie. He thought he saw a coffee mug in the background. Asians were always building ridiculous-shaped buildings like that. The casualty reports on the tattered paper were far grimmer.

"They lost at least as many as us," General Lewis said as if that counted this as a victory. "We'll just enlist more muties to fight."

Each mission they planned, every raid by the mutie soldiers, was fruitless, even with their best intelligence reports. The casualties were always comparable, never giving one side a leg up over the other. As promising as they seemed, each one went off like a flash in the pan.

"We've been at this war for twenty years," she said, voice hoarse but full of longing. "Can't we call a truce with the enemy and work to rebuild?"

"We're not giving up before they do," Lewis said.

"I'll eat algae bars till my skin turns green," McDuncan tacked on.

General Kane looked at his advisors. They'd all been young men when they retreated into these bunkers with the rest of those who could get here in time. Mostly well-connected people that could fly there before the first bombs went off. Now they were older than their former commanders, with a dwindling population due to poor nutrition.

"We're committed to ending the war," General Kane recited, "we will repair what's broken when we can rebuild the whole world in our image." It was the company line, the motto of the generals that led these bunkers before him. He hoped it'd be the motto of those who survived him.

"If you're still committed to staying down here then is there anything you need from us?" she asked, strength returning to her voice now that she'd finished the water. It was probably the finest cup of water she'd ever had, even if it had been run through the recycling process a few dozen times this month.

"A mutie, offering *us* help," General McDuncan scoffed.

Kane cut him off with a hand wave before he said anything worse. Times were hard on everyone. At least they had lead shielding to block out the worst of the radiation. "We appreciate your support and efforts on the air, ground, and sea. We will be sending up a fresh supply of algae bars for you and the troops. It's not as much as normal. Times are tough." Looking at her disfigured face, he didn't think he needed to remind her.

The generals questioned her about a few more operations, and she reported on them diligently. She was as knowledgeable as any of them but polite enough to remind McDuncan and Lewis about specific details of the operations they'd "misremembered." She would have made a great general if she had made it to the bunker in time. But now she gave off radiation like a socialist gave out food stamps. It was too much a risk to keep her down here. He had to use everyone as best he could in times like these.

After planning a few more strikes on their enemies, they sent her away with almost a dozen crates of algae bars from their hydroponic systems. The lieutenant led her to the elevator shaft that connected their bunker to the harsh irradiated world.

*\*\*\**

Jonah stepped off the elevator shaft and into the fresh air of the bunker's upstairs lobby. She scratched the tumor on her neck. The dingy recycled air of the bunkers always made her feel like she was drowning. The bunker's lobby was full of miniature models of each major city the generals had launched a strike against. It was cheaper than sending out actual bombs.

"How'd it go?" Li-An asked. She was seated in her wheelchair near a model of Rio De Janeiro using her mobile hand to play with the Christ the Redeemer figurine.

"Same as always," Jonah sighed, stepping off the lift and pulling the neck tumor off, "these prosthetics get more uncomfortable every time."

"What should we do with these crates?" an aide asked.

"Put them in storage with the rest. I think we're turning them into fertilizer these days," Jonah said with a wave of her left hand. A sore fell off it and landed on the ground with a wet *whap*. She was worried about that one and tried to keep it in her pocket the whole meeting. "How did things go with your chairmen?" she asked Li An, a best friend she'd never have if the bunker-heads had their way.

"Requested pictures of the attack on Las Vegas," she said, words cruising smoothly out of her half-paralyzed mouth. "I showed them some doctored pictures of babies with congenital disabilities, and they encouraged us to breed it out of our systems."

"I'm extremely confident that's not how that works," Jonah said with a chuckle. She took a seat in the makeup room and pulled the rest of the prosthetics off.

"It'd also mean I wouldn't have gotten to meet Fred and other fellow patients in my physical therapy group. And I don't know what I'd do without them," Li An added.

"Fred's great! It would be terrible if we didn't know him," Jonah lamented. "Hey, did they care that the cars in Las Vegas had the same license plates as the cars we used in the New York model?"

"No," Li-An said, unconcerned. "I think they were just happy to see the Las Vegas sign stabbed into the sphinx."

"The modelers do have their fun with it. I think there was a coffee mug in the background of mine. They didn't say anything."

The pair left the office, the crates of algae bars gone as well. They took a high-speed monorail down the East Coast to meet Fundiswa for lunch. They'd picked a barbecue place in Montgomery to meet at, and it was a bit of a commute to get there. But the pair filled the thirty minutes discussing the exciting Mars landing New Delhi had just completed.

"You ever feel bad for not telling them?" Li-An asked as they made their way through the line, picking out which smoked slaughter-free meats they wanted for lunch.

"I offered to help them," Jonah said. "It's not like we locked them down there. There was that one guy who came up years ago."

"Yeah, that's right. He didn't believe his eyes," Li-An said after taking a moment to remember the past years.

"He kept trying to figure out what we were hiding. Eventually, we built a set and hired actors so he could expose our lies and return underground."

Jonah carried their trays past the unattended cash register, a decorative relic that matched the restaurant's old-timey aesthetic, and found their friend Fundiswa halfway done with their meal.

After short greetings and cutting the brisket into bite-size pieces for her friend, Jonah asked the question that had been on her mind since they decided to meet for lunch. "How's Noxolo doing?" Unfortunately, some tumors were real up here.

Fundiswa sighed. "She's getting better. The doctors are hopeful that she will recover soon."

"Is she tired often?" Li-An asked.

"Here and there, but the new medicine they're using isn't as bad as it used to be."

"I don't know how I would have made it through my stroke without them," Li-An said after finishing her bite. Jonah still didn't know how Li An did it with the new medical tech; she'd pulled off more than Jonah could imagine.

"How much longer are you going to be in this hemisphere?" Jonah eventually asked.

"I'm flying back after this. Her parents are cooking us dinner, and I've got to be in town to meet with the ministers tomorrow."

"Oh yeah," Jonah said, pulling a portfolio out of her bag. "Here are the images of London they'll want."

Fundiswa cracked the file open. "This is awful."

"Did they leave something in the background?" Jonah asked, concerned.

"No, just the destruction they want to see." Fundiswa seemed as if the faux bombs had landed at their feet. "If they weren't already locked down, I'd want them imprisoned."

"I'm just glad we loaded blanks before they put in the launch codes," Li-An said with her joyful and meandering smile.

Jonah was glad someone made that call every day. She enjoyed their lunch at the wooden picnic table under the sunset tint of the LED lights. Over the speakers, a new country artist sang about seeing their hometown twinkle from orbit. She hoped to take another vacation to the stars soon and see the full-sized cities intact. The planet's dark side looked like light caught in a diamond on her last trip. She hoped her blue world would continue to shine for a long time to come.

# Escaping the Butcher's Pit

Published June 3, 2022 - StepIntoTheRoad.com

H ow did I get here? It's not how you'd expect.

Woah, be careful where you point that thing!

Most people take starships to get places or underground transit in more industrialized worlds. Horses are a tried and true transport for galactic colonists worried about their next meal and their EV's next charge. I've taken them all at one point or another, But to get here, I came through a womb, like most mammalian beasts and some alien beasts, as long as you don't hold too strict a definition.

I came from my father's womb, born on a distant planet where everything was legal. My parents fled there to be themselves. Who could blame them? But with no laws, the powerful let the horrors in their hearts leech into the world. Being ourselves under their looming towers did little to protect us.

My fathers provided what they could for as long as they could. Unfortunately, like many people on our planet, they disappeared into the darkness one night. Captured by some dark pursuit or lured into a trap set by others.

As an orphaned boy, a generous butcher adopted me. She wasn't the kind of butcher that sliced into cattle or alien reptiles. Kids were what she maimed. Not with knives but with explosives. The lot of us under her care worked the mines. We squeezed into gaps grown men couldn't reach. We set handmade explosives and sifted through the rubble for anything she might find valuable. The fingers of my right hand were lost one day, never to be recovered since they didn't fetch a price in the butcher's market.

I was considered a man when I no longer fit into the cracks and crevices despite being a few years shy of 18. The city's terror and lures were advertised to me as I searched for a shelter to sleep under each night. I wonder if one of my fathers is sitting comfortably in a high tower. He had an uncanny knack for getting his way. I have no doubt the one who nurtured me for nine months and another nine years fell victim to one of the city's many cruelties.

To escape the dangers of the night, I joined the navy. They were happy to forge the paperwork for the extra credits that came with my recruitment. I did not know the dangers service held in and of itself. Their training was no worse than the butcher's beatings and berating. They provided me with two nutritious meals a day and one new bionic hand. They'll likely want back if they ever catch me.

Once assigned to the powerful warship Mafaldine — yes, the one you just faced off against.

The captain and crew were more interested in the comforts of the Central System than bringing pirates and smugglers to justice. They'd attack you all the same, but the justice you saw at the end of their blasters was far from what the judges of the Central System intended. From the captain's perspective, extra comforts and credits were due to us, especially if the haul was twice the listed bounty. I learned that a few additional credits went far on the frontier worlds where we occasionally stopped. And I saw that laws did little to hinder corruption. They merely produce hoops too high for us little guys to jump through.

I soon found I had more in common with the captured criminals than the crew. They were just people from homeworlds like mine. Many were living on a ship that didn't have the blessing of the Navy. Soon I put my mining experience to good use and lay homemade explosives through the lower corridors of the Mafaldine.

Surely you didn't think your rail guns were what opened the stock rooms into the void of space. I slipped onto this ship in the chaos of repairs and fighting. I hope that, despite the laser cutlasses singing my neck hairs, you'll consider how that encounter might have gone without my help.

Sure, you could have handled it. The world turned us into capable fighters. How else would we claw our way out of the pit we were born into? I hope to serve on this honest crew of pirates. Since only a criminal genuinely acts out the role society wrote for us.

# Bum Thumb

Published December 20, 2023 - Orbs of Purpose & Other Fantastical Stories

My thumb was black and swollen I had busted it catching a pop fly while I was playing outfielder on our Sunday afternoon game.

I wanted to quit playing. I came back to the bench and showed Coach Robin how black and blue it was. I thought if I put it into the glove it would swell more and I'd never be able to get the thing off.

I thought this was going to be fatal. Not fatal to my life, you can live with a broken thumb. Our neighbor Mr. Pachinski lives fine without a thumb at all. But it would be fatal to my dream of becoming a millionaire ball player. That's what I spent all the rest of my time in the outfield thinking about. Nothing else came for me and we wound up losing the game. But it wasn't my fault. I hit all the balls I could, unfortunately, I hadn't been given any good pitches.

I thought about how I'd never become a famous ball player from that moment to the end of the X-ray after the game. Turns out that the the thumb was just jammed a bit and the bone was fine. It was bruised but if I put some ice on it I'd be fine.

When it got home it turned out that we didn't have any ice made. My mom put some into the fridge and handed me a paper towel that had something solid and cold in it.

"What's this mom?"

"Fish," she replied.

"Gross! I can't put raw fish on my hand."

"It's fine! The cod is vacuum sealed and frozen. You know how that ice takes forever to freeze." She explained with a mild amount of sympathy.

"I don't know if I can make it to practice tomorrow," I said as I sat on the couch. She turned on the TV, some news channel about the next political travesty or drama.

"You can make it to practice you'll be fine. You're a fighter." The words in the statement were genuine but I knew she was being sarcastic. She flipped the channel from one news station to another. That one was complaining about how things weren't going very well either, it went on and on about some missile crisis or another. I got up and took my frozen fish up to my room where I'd be able to watch whatever game was on tonight or I'd put in an awesome action movie like The Scorpion King.

The next morning my room smelled awful. I had messed up and never put the fish back into the freezer. It thawed and quit helping my thumb after I fell asleep and I left it in my bed. The vacuum seal wasn't as good as mom had thought and there was a small puddle of fish juice in the middle of my bed. It look like someone had carelessly jacked off. It reminded me of the scene in that one movie where the guy found a horse head in his bed.

I told Mom about it, I was already too late for school to deal with it, and she'd have to get to it before work. Luckily the ice had frozen and I had something that wouldn't smell for the bus ride to school.

After school, walking towards the baseball field that was as far away from the school building as possible my neck sweat from the heat of the late May sun. It'd be a hot summer. I'd still play baseball, there was no doubt about it that, our season would last well into the summer since we were playing so well. But I'd be hot the entire time. Maybe if we were lucky coach would push practice back and we'd play under the field's light and the moon. Evening practice wasn't always colder, the Texas humidity cloaked the heat onto the field until well into the night, but it was cooler.

When I got to the dugout it was clear Coach wasn't pushing practice back. He was a veteran catcher of the Dragons, a small A-minus league that no one had heard of unless they had met him. Then he's talking your ear off about it.

His favorite game to talk about was when he played the Leprechauns. He convinced his pitcher to throw his signature laser fastball. Catching the ball wasn't hard, but it was so fast it'd pop his glove into his chest. But it never failed to strike the Leprechaun batters out.

The problem was that the balls were fast and it wore his deep brown glove to a light copper. Worst of all it turned out that it was damaging Coach's wrist. From the fifth inning on each time Coach caught a ball he had to ignore a spike of pain in his wrist. In the end, the Dragons won but Coach went to the hospital afterwards and the lab results said he'd have to sit out the rest of the season.

I hoped my thumb injury wouldn't do the same to me. I wanted to be able to play in the major leagues, instead of topping out at some minor minor minor league like coach.

I pulled my glove over my damaged thumb and grimaced as it pulled over my damaged hand.

"Coach I don't think I can practice today."

"Cause of your thumb?" He asked, I could tell it was rhetorical.

"Yeah."

"Well if you can't practice you can't play."

"I'll be fine by the end of the week. I'll be good for the next game."

"You'll be healed sure. But you'll be a week out of practice. If ya don't want to practice that's fine. Write your name on the absence log and go home." He gestured to the dusty clipboard that always hung at the end of the dugout. "It'll just mean you're benched next week."

Sometimes coach could be a real asshole. I could use a pencil on the log and erase it before the end of the week. There was so much going on that Coach would forget that I ever skipped practice. That's why he had the log but he didn't guard it like a dragon's hoard.

I walked over to it. Took it off its rusty nail of a hook. My glove was on by my hand but it hurt.

I looked at the names, mostly seniors who'd gotten scholarships but not to any notable colleges. Wondered what this meant on my path towards the majors and staying in fancy hotels at away games.

I hung the clipboard back up and walked out to the field. My thumb throbbed in my glove but there was cod at home to ice it with after practice.

# Anthony's Apprenticeship

Published March 23, 2018 -
StepIntoTheRoad.com

"**A**nt! Get over here!" Lorent's impatient assistant shouted through the hallways of the stone temple to get Anthony's attention.

In a room down the hall, Anthony scrambled to put his quill safely above his workspace where it would not get ink on the parchment he was copying. He walked as quickly as would still be considered polite to Lorent's office. Piena, the assistant, was sitting in Lorent's chair, at Lorent's desk, looking over Lorent's paperwork, as usual.

"Yes sir, how can I help you?" The boy said between pants.

Piena looked over the edge of the scrolls he was examining and smiled at the young boy. "Lorent is going to be traveling to Makenza to meet with his order of Holy Shepherds. He needs you to make preparations for the journey."

"Yes sir," Anthony replied. He got the necessary information from the assistant and turned to head out the door.

Then Piena said, "And one more thing Ant." The boy turned around, "You got a letter today." The assistant waved his hand, and a small parchment floated off the desk and towards the boy. He snatched it out of the air once it was close enough. "Unfortunately it's not good news." A devilish smile danced across the assistant's face.

The first thing Anthony noticed was not who it was from but that the seal had already been broken. Anthony bared a grin at the man behind the desk and said, "Thank you."

The gods gave out many gifts in Anthony's world. Some, like people like Lorent, were given the gift of significant magic. Lorent could heal others of almost any trauma. Lorent was a cleric belonging to the order of the Holy Shepherd. The gods gave others minor magical abilities. Piena was one of these people and could move things with his mind but could not perform tremendous feats. Most people had this level of magical ability. Others, like Anthony, had no magical abilities at all. Some would say he was cursed and none of the gods had given him favor. And while all evidence pointed to this being true, the boy still had some gifts.

These gifts weren't given to him by the gods, at least not directly like magic was. These gifts were given to him by his mother. He could read and write his letters and combine the numbers doing sums and arithmetic. These were gifts his mother, who had once been a priestess, had taught him.

He now used them to serve the cleric Lorent as a scribe and secretary. Healing was a time and energy-consuming task for the cleric. For food, water, shelter, and a continued education Anthony served the holy man by planning all travel and transposing the man's many scrolls and documents. Anthony took the job because with it he could send money to his mother and father. But that wasn't his only motivation. He also dreamed that Lorent could cure his lack of magical abilities.

Unfortunately, in the past five years of service, the man hadn't said a word to Anthony.

Anthony sat back down at his small table in the study and unfolded the letter he had received. It was from his mother, but he didn't have to read the signature to know that. Of the two people in the world who cared about him, she was the only parent who could write.

*Sweet Anthony,*

*I hope this letter finds you well. I am low on ink so I must be brief. The crops are filling in, but they are not as plentiful as we had hoped. Your father says this is because he has been unable to work them every day. I have had to assure him that it is merely a rough season. He has failed to work in the field because his health has been leaving him. I have done what I can with the few herbs and medicines I have, but it has not done much for him.*

*I have no desire to distract you from your apprenticeship or your studies, but if you can find the time to steal away and visit your father, it would do wonders for his fading heart.*

*Love always,*

*Father & Mother*

The ink of the letter produced a gradient on the page. The boy's name was in jet-black ink, but by the time the signature came, the lettering was made with an empty grey. He held the paper at an angle to the light and saw that the last two letters were not written in ink but had been lightly scratched in. She had continued to write the final letters without any ink.

Anthony reread the note until he understood his mother's meaning. His father was dying, but she didn't have the heart to tell him. Unfortunately, with Lorent's trip to Makenza coming up there would be no way for him to visit them.

He cursed the gods as he had many times before under many different circumstances. His father was too young for death in Anthony's mind. The boy had always dreamed that once he became an assistant for the cleric, he would be able to move his parents into the halls of the assistant so they wouldn't have to work the farm in their old age.

He had pitched the idea to Piena before since the man had no living relatives himself, but the assistant just snorted and told him that he would rather have the rooms empty than filled with peasants.

Anthony had retorted with a comment about how when he became an assistant he would show the Holy Shepherd's love by filling all empty rooms with people who needed them. Unfortunately, this leads to Piena continually mocking him about his dream of becoming an assistant. At every turn, Piena stopped the boy from showing his few abilities off to Lorent or any person of mention. It was after that point that Anthony quit sharing his dreams with anyone.

He sat and thought about the information his mother sent him. Anthony mourned his father's sickness but steeled himself against grief that would stop him from doing work. Then he pulled out scrolls, maps, and timetables off of the shelves of the study. His mind went to work at what it did best. Anthony began making travel plans for more than one party.

By the wee hours of the morning, and many candles later, he had three things: an inkling of hope for his father's recovery, a clear map for Lorent's journey, and a letter to his mother that he would have to send without Piena finding it.

\*\*\*

Three days later Lorent and his caravan set out for Makenza following the path Anthony had set for them. It would take them five days to get to the city. The group was small. It contained three minor priests who followed the cleric and a boy younger than Anthony whose parents had paid Lorent for his safe passage.

The first day of travel was uneventful. Anthony started the morning early, packed the cleric's bags, and prepared the animals for the trip. He double-checked that the scrolls Lorent requested were stored safely in a small waterproof chest. Anthony packed the food, medicine, and other supplies carefully on the mule-drawn cart.

The company left the temple an hour after sunrise, ahead of schedule thanks to Anthony's preparations. The rest of that day was uneventful, and they made camp in the evening at a spot Anthony found on an old map. Around the campfire, Lorent remarked to the group that he felt great spiritual energy in the place.

Piena replied, "Thank you, my lord. I made sure to find a place that would suit you." Anthony stayed quiet.

The next morning Anthony awoke before sunrise, prepared the company's breakfast, and loaded the supplies that had been used at camp back onto the animals. As he did this, he overheard a conversation between Lorent and his assistant.

"I had a dream from the Shepherd last night," Lorent said in an inconspicuous tone. "She was warning me that this journey is being used for selfish purposes."

"Hmmm," Piena replied with interest. Anthony's forehead began to sweat despite the cool morning breeze. "Did the goddess mention who was manipulating the voyage?"

"No," Lorent replied, "That part she did not reveal to me, the future is still not clear. You are the only one who knows this. We must stay vigilant and keep the young boy who is in our care safe. His mother paid me well to lead him to Makenza safely."

"Of course of course," the assistant said.

"I will consult my priests individually to see if the goddess blessed them with any knowledge that I do not have. Maybe she will reveal which one of them may be behind this."

"That seems very wise indeed my lord," Piena replied.

The conversation ended, and Anthony quickly got back to work wondering how he would handle being found out by Lorent.

***

Anthony was on edge the entire second day of travel, but no one approached him with the subject. Lorent was as stoic as ever, and if he hadn't heard their conversation, the boy would have never expected the cleric to be on to his plans.

On the third day of travel, no one had approached Anthony about the potential deceit, and he had all but forgotten about it until the end of the day.

Lorent was leading the caravan and consulting one of his priests as the party approached a fork in the road. The cleric halted the party and Piena came to the front. Anthony followed with the map of the journey.

"Which way do we proceed Piena?" Lorent asked.

"To the right my lord," the assistant said without consulting Anthony.

Anthony spoke up in a meek tone, "Actually sirs, I planned for us to go left."

Both men looked at him surprised. Anthony presented the map. It showed that both ways led to Makenza, and the right path was undoubtedly shorter. Piena pointed out this much and looked down his nose to challenge Anthony to disagree.

"I admit the right is a shorter path, but it is through the mountains and will be hard on the animals. The left path was longer but smoother, and I made sure that we left with enough time. This way will get us to Makenza with plenty of time and the horses, not to mention we, will be fresher when we arrive."

Piena scoffed in disagreement. "You are wasting all of our time with this." He turned to Lorent for agreement. "Lord, which direction should we take?"

The cleric looked at the horizon. The sun was about to set. "It sounds like we have time regardless of the path we take. Let us make camp here for the evening, and you two can settle the decision between yourselves." Lorent dismounted his horse and led them to a clearing to make camp.

Anthony proceeded to prepare food for the evening and cooked for everyone as usual. Piena didn't bring up the situation of which path to take and by the time dishes from dinner were finished Anthony had no energy to argue with the assistant. The group went to bed around the embers of the fire.

Late in the night, Anthony was shaken awake. The boy gasped for air, but a hand covered his mouth. His eyes adjusted to the darkness and he saw Piena looming over him. "Look Ant," the man spat, "I don't know how you found out about my plan, but I won't let you ruin it. We're taking the mountain road so the thugs I hired can take care of Lorent."

Anthony's eyes grew wide in shock, "Mrmmr," he said through his muffled mouth. He didn't know anything about Piena's plot, but now that he did he wasn't going to let Piena get away with it. He tried to cry out again but couldn't make a sound. Piena held the boy still and silent with both his hands. Then the evil assistant used his magic to levitate his knife out of its sheath. The blade floated from his waist to Anthony's throat. He felt the sharp metal press against his neck.

"You know, no one would notice if you were gone. I wouldn't even have to hide your dead body very well. Lorent wouldn't even remember you if you disappeared."

"You're a useless little non-magic boy," the man continued. "Your only talent is being able to write and plan, and even that you seem to mess up. Well, this time it's going to cost you your life."

"No, it won't." A voice came from the darkness. A sword was unsheathed and illuminated the campsite with its light. The sword lit up its wielder's face. Lorent was standing in front of the boy and the assistant. Slowly the rest of the camp started to wake up in the commotion.

The knife that was magically held at Anthony's throat dropped to the ground as Piena lost concentration on it.

"I dreamt that someone was tricking me and going to betray me." Lorent said, "Then I heard the scream of a boy in my mind. I woke up and heard your whispering carried through the night. You were the one that planned to betray this caravan."

By this time the cleric's followers were surrounding Piena and the boy. "Tie him up and we will carry him to the authorities in Makenza."

The assistant looked at the knife that was lying on the ground. He tried to move it, but Anthony put his small hand on the hilt. He felt it struggle in his hand, but Anthony fought Piena's magical powers. Then a priest put his hands over the assistant's eyes and put him into a deep magical sleep.

***

The next day they took the long path around the mountain as Anthony had suggested. Halfway through the day's travels, they came across a man and woman waiting on the side of the road. The man was young but looked sick and weak. The woman appeared tired from helping him on their journey. As Lorent approached them, he halted the caravan to see if he could provide aid.

The cleric approached the couple. "I see you are tired and sick, is there anything I can do to help?" He asked.

"You are kind sir," the woman responded, "Our son mentioned that if the gods were good, we might be able to find you on this road. We were hard-pressed to get here quick enough, but it seems we were blessed."

"Your son, how did he know?" Lorent looked at the woman confused.

Then Anthony trotted up on his small pony, and his mother smiled at him. After he got down, they embraced, and he greeted his father who was seated on the ground propped against a rock. The man was pale from his fading heart.

"Sir Lorent. I have not been entirely truthful." Anthony began to explain. "We took the longer path so that I could see my father once more before he passed. I knew that I would not be able to leave your service to see him so I thought I could meet him on the road. I'm sorry that I hid this from you."

Lorent let out a wondrous laugh, "Boy you could not be more wrong. I am grateful that we took this longer path for it saved my life." The cleric squatted to inspect the old man. He looked at Anthony's mother and asked what was wrong. After hearing the diagnosis, he told one of his priests to fetch specific herbs and medicines from the cart.

Lorent prepared a potion and changed a spell to help the father. By the end of the short break at the side of the road, the man was able to stand up. "Here are some spare herbs." Lorent said, addressing Anthony's mother, "Please give them to him as you see fit, he should be better in a week."

"Thank you, sir," she responded. "Is there anything we can do to repay you?"

Lorent smiled, "No your son has been enough of a blessing to me. Is there anything else we can do for you? Do you need supplies for the way back home?"

"No there's nothing," the woman responded.

"Actually, there is one thing," Anthony said interrupting. His parents and Lorent looked down at the small boy. "If you wouldn't mind sir, I was hoping we could give my mother more ink so that she could write me. She ran out writing me the last letter about my father."

"Do we have any extra?" Lorent asked one of his priests. The priest shrugged not knowing.

"Yes, we do," Anthony said, "I brought an extra vial," the young man produced a small black bottle out of his satchel.

"Of course you did," Lorent said with a smile. He took the bottle out of the boy's hand and passed it on to the mother. "Please write to him as often as you can. But more importantly, come visit."

"Thank you sir, but we could never intrude like that," the mother protested.

"Nonsense," the cleric rebuffed, "Your son is my assistant now since the last one has been so dishonest. Your son has an honest soul, and as the assistant, he has extra rooms for his family at our temple. Please come join us when your husband is healthy enough to travel."

"Assistant?" The mother said in shock. She looked at Anthony for clarification, but he was as confused as her.

"Your son has served me loyally for years. He has learned a lot from his texts and from watching me. He may never have magic powers but he has an honest heart, and that is far more valuable than magic." Lorent looked down at the boy. "That is if you will be willing to work with me and continue the work of the Holy Sheperd."

Anthony beamed with admiration. The midday sun illuminated his hero. Anthony replied boldly, "Thank you, sir. I would be honored to serve you and the Sheperd."

# Creative Autopilot

Published August 3, 2018 -
StepIntoTheRoad.com

I was contacted recently by a reader who found themselves in a peculiar situation. His name is Jeremiah Trout, or at least that's the name he prefers to go by. After verifying his claims as best I could I decided that his story fit the theme of this blog. He agreed to let me share it with you, and I'm glad.

Jeremiah, like myself, has always wanted to be a writer. However, one of the first things he said to me was, "I fear I don't possess a creative bone in my body." I assure you, reader, by the end of this tale you will, as I do, believe very differently.

Mr. Trout's troubles began when he received an email informing him that a short story he submitted to a reputable online publisher accepted the piece and would be publishing it on their site within the month. The publisher transferred the funds automatically and the rights to the story, unbeknownst to Jeremiah, were no longer his. This is why we should read the terms and services, ladies and gentlemen.

While most writers, myself included, would be thrilled to have a story accepted and would take it as an indicator we were on the right path, Jeremiah became frantic. See, he had only submitted the story as a sort of litmus test of his potential. He never expected it to be accepted let alone bought.

Jeremiah had made the grievous error of submitting a story that was not his. He didn't commit the sin of full-on plagiarism, but he wrote to the publisher that they could not publish the story because it was not wholly his to sell.

They loved the story or at the very least required something for their deadline and they pushed Jeremiah to inform them of who wrote the story so they could publish it. Jeremiah proceeded to explain that his computer had written it.

"Of course it was written on a computer," they replied, "We didn't expect you to have a typewriter in this day and age."

Jeremiah, in an effort to clear up the matter, insisted, "I afraid you misunderstood me. My computer wrote it... itself." He went slightly deeper and explained that he had created an artificial intelligence of sorts that wrote short stories automatically. Ending the explanation, he said, "I submitted a few of the half-way decent ones to publishers."

The publisher scoffed at the description of "half-way decent" and demanded proof of Jeremiah's creation. Luckily, Jeremiah didn't send over his software putting all of us aspiring writers out of business and quickly lining the pockets of all those distributing tales of fiction. However, He did send over a few copies of the computer's earlier works. He sent me the same things when we started our correspondence.

I would say I read them, but that would be a lie. These documents were unreadable. They were only a tad better than an infinite number of monkeys trying to write the complete works of Shakespear. Any first-year computer science major could write a random word generator that had a better plot than these stories.

Despite these early signs of hopelessness Jeremiah persevered. He researched story writing and programming, and he looked for solutions to making a program that might be more creative than him. At first, it was slow progress. He found countless bugs but continued to fix them. After what seemed like endless changes to the neural network he eventually had an artificial intelligence that worked. Mr. Trout's machine had begun to put together a passable story. Then with some feedback, more computing power, and the ever-valuable asset of time, the computer started to create works that the inventor thought were decent. I've read some of these, and I will admit, I had a hard time putting them down, a sentiment I assume the publisher shared.

The publisher was ecstatic once they heard that this nearly endless supply of stories was available. They offered Jeremiah funding to pursue his project further and an open forum to share all of the computer's tales.

However, the promise of money for the machine was a blow to Jeremiah's ego. He knew that he would never be able to write with half the talent of the device. When he did sit down to write, like most writers, it took him forever to get started. Moreover, even when he struck a vein inspiration, it would never hold up after a second reading. Trout's hopes were dashed before he had gotten any traction. This was when he concluded that he didn't have a single creative bone in his body. Of course, if he were genuinely uncreative, then he wouldn't be having any of the problems he was facing.

The publisher ran the story despite Trout's wishes for them to redact it. Since Jeremiah didn't write the story, they didn't give him credit as the author. Instead, they gave the machine a pseudonym I've forgotten, but they did put an asterisk next to the name and added as a footnote that the near genius and a man ahead of his time, Jeremiah Trout had discovered the author.

Maybe this was a political move in an effort to soothe Jeremiah's ego and encourage him to sell them more stories. However, there is something to be said for someone who has created such an awe-inspiring program.

I hope one day Jeremiah will start the program back up and spin some fantastic tales for the world to read. At the very least I've encouraged him to continue to keep the pen wet and to write even if he feels like everything he makes is garbage. However, after meeting with him and getting a feel for his personality, I am sure he's already trying his hand at engineering something even more magnificent than a computer that writes short stories.

# Rose Colored Glasses

Published December 29, 2017 -
StepIntoTheRoad.com

U nfortunately for you, Reader, I can't tell you from where this story came. The weird thing about hosting a small site on the vast Internet is that you get some very strange visitors. Every once and a while someone fills out the "contact me" page and I get a fascinating tale from a passing onlooker. Jerome, the main character of this story was kind enough to let me share the story with all of you on this site. I thought you might find his invention of reality-augmenting rose-colored glasses as interesting as I did.

Jerome Balquin is a single father and an avid hobbyist. For his day job, which most of us have despite our best efforts, he is an engineer at a company that is far too large. When this whole situation took place about three years ago he was down on his luck. His wife passed away a few years before, and the company he worked for was "strategically reorganizing" a well-known code for constant layoffs.

In his garage, he tinkers, and he decided to try his hand at augment-ed reality. With some well-placed code and fascinating optics that even

I'm astounded by, he created what he calls the Rose Colored Glasses. They do what you would expect, everything he sees through them is absolutely positive.

His overdue bills looked like love letters from his lost sweetheart. Instead of reading failing test grades on his son's schoolwork, he saw the teacher's praise him for being a fabulous father. Best of all the pile of half-finished inventions now sat on his workbench in their full working glory ready to be sold to help him escape his job. Jerome, for once, was thrilled by the invention.

Unfortunately, he couldn't justify living in this augmented world. He left the glasses to rust on his workbench expecting to only pick them up in time of deep depression.

A few weeks later he came home from a particularly rough day at work, on top of that his son had brought home a report card. He wanted the glasses to keep his son's grades from seeming too lousy. Yet, he had no luck finding the glasses. Without their aid, he opened up the report card and was unsurprised to see nothing higher than a C.

He walked into the living room prepared to have a chat with his son about the atrocious grades. "Hamil," he addressed the boy, "we need to talk about these grades."

The young teenager looked up at him and beamed. "Aren't you proud Dad?" He asked.

Jerome reexamined the grades thinking he had missed something. "You aren't serious?" The father scoffed.

"Yeah, I am! I looked at them before I gave them to you and they were all above a C unlike usual. Also, Mr. Reinhart returned my English paper with a raving note." The boy pulled a neatly folded essay out of his bag.

Jerome unfolded the essay and read the red script at the top "F incompetent understanding of the subject and the language as a whole."

Then he scanned through a dozen grammar and spelling errors his son had made. He looked back up at his son who was carefully studying a social studies textbook at the kitchen table.

Confused, the father examined the grades and his studying son. He admitted it took him too long to put things together. However, he finally figured out that his son was the one who had filched the spectacles. He decided to let the sleeping pup lie since his son was eagerly studying at the kitchen table.

Things went along like this for a few weeks until Jerome got a call from his son's teacher. "Mr. Balquin," the teacher started, "I'd like to talk to you about your son's very peculiar habits in school."

"What seems to be the problem?" He replied. Calls like this weren't rare. His son often misbehaved in class.

"He refuses to do any work without a particular set of glasses on. Does he have vision problems?"

Jerome could have cut his losses and simply lied to get out of the whole situation. However, through my conversations with the fellow, I can tell you he is an honest man and lying isn't in his character.

Instead, our inventor friend said, "Well Mrs. Reinhart, his glasses help him see the positive side of things. He studies better with them, so I encouraged him to keep wearing them at school."

"The positive side of things?" The teacher scoffed. "Your son takes tests and does most of our in-class assignments wearing them. He is constantly answering questions, most of the time wrong, but he doesn't seem to care."

"How are his grades?" Jerome asked.

"He hasn't made anything higher than a B all semester. And while he completes every assignment, most of the time they are so far from correct I can't understand why he continues to put so much effort into the assignments."

The father hummed in thought. I'm sure any reader who was a student, no matter how atrocious, will realize that a low grade is far more valuable than a zero to your overall GPA. Jerome replied, "I'm sorry that he is still answering questions incorrectly. We are doing our very best at home to study every night." His son had been nagging him to study every night because of the encouragement his teacher gave him.

"I assume there isn't any problem with him continuing to use the eyeglasses in class," Jerome asked the teacher.

"Hamil tells me that it doesn't connect to wifi or any other kind of internet," The teacher stated, "I wanted to make sure that was true because it's so hard to tell what these kids' technology can and can't do these days."

"The glasses do nothing of the sort," Jerome assured her, "They are not giving him any answers. His continued poor grades can assure you of that." The man said this with a chuckle hoping the teacher would lighten up.

"Very well sir," the teacher said, "I see no issue with letting him continue to use them. I am sorry that I have had to call you with such disturbing and ill news about your son's studiousness, but I'm sure with some time he will finish high school, or the GED, and get a promising job as a janitor."

"Thank you very much, Mrs. Reinhart," Jerome replied with a smile, "I'm glad that you took the time to fill me in on how my son was doing in class."

Jerome explained to me that this conversation was an indication his son was on the right track. He says that young Hamil has been far more studious over the past few years since he stumbled upon the glasses.

When I inquired about what happened with the lenses and if Hamil still uses them Jerome informed me that he made a more conspicuous pair so that Hamil wouldn't catch any more flack from his teachers. Hamil is now a junior in high school. He has aced both his SAT and ACT exams and has applied to a handful of Ivy League colleges. The father says Hamil has already received an acceptance letter from some. The boy plans to dual major in astrophysics and applied mathematics to the excitement of his father.

Jerome himself keeps me updated from time to time about how his glasses are improving. He hopes to bring his augmented reality design to market in the next few years. So far he has a few angel investors who have enabled him to quit his job. He now pursues his invention full-time.

If you have a student, who isn't doing too well in school or have a boss that you want to quit reading nagging emails from, then keep an eye out for Jerome's rose-colored glasses. And if someone seems to be having a great day despite how dreary the world around them is ask them about how they do it. They might be a Beta Tester of Jerome's new invention.

# Swinging Sticks

Published September 1, 2022 - Path of the
Bearers and Other Stories

The house they put me in was just this side of falling apart. I'd had nicer apartments and worse ones. It was still serviceable, but if I didn't get done what I'd come here to do, I would wind up becoming a repairman, not something I was well suited for.

The house sat in a place outside of time and space. It had taken me nearly a decade to save up enough money to get here, and I had one purpose: write and finish at least one great novel. Which I would soon find was not as simple as I'd originally expected.

The first floor had a sitting room, void of a television and radio, but plenty of paintings on the walls. Although they were too realistic for my liking. The pantry was stocked with countless canned foods and staples that were bound to last a lifetime. The refrigerator had no shortage of fresh options available to me there.

When I walked up the stairs, the second step from the top creaked every time I stepped on it, and the sound echoed through the vacuous house. There were two bedrooms on the second floor, neither of which were large. One held a single bed, a dresser with black and gray shirts, and a nightstand with a small stained glass lamp on it.

The room across the hall held a heavy wooden desk with ornate carvings from the clawed feet to the vines that seemed to grow around the edges. The polished wood top was vacant with the exception of an old-fashioned typewriter. No embedded terminal, no microphone for voice transcribing; they didn't even go as low tech as an ancient desktop computer tower. The typewriter didn't plug into the wall and couldn't connect to a network, even if there was one in this pocket dimension. The drawers held a number of pens, pencils, quills, and paintbrushes. A few reams of paper sat in the bottom desk drawer, the sturdy wood unwilling to buckle under the weight of the paper.

A bookshelf loomed behind the desk, carved just as intricately. The books, most of which I'd requested to be there for reference or inspiration, had genuine paper pages with stiff covers. A shelf alone would have covered the cost of my entrance into this place. And I let the thin pages flutter across my thumb as I looked them over.

Vogelfonte Inc. specializes in the creation, maintenance, and transportation to sub-dimensional pockets of existence. It was proprietary technology that Augustus Vogelfonte discovered, and its usage varies from military training to creative retreats and is marketed to multiple sectors and conglomerates that are interested in advancement and improvement. No one outside the company knows how it works, least of all me, a writer of, at best, space station dramas.

Until recently, I worked as a logistical engineer for the Acrecia conglomerate, which handled the food distribution to most major systems. It was about as creative a pursuit as buff-cow herding, and even then, I may not be giving the ranchers enough credit. It paid me just a little more than my expenses, but I worked to stash away enough to take out a loan on a Vogelfonte sub-dimensional creative retreat. I got a discount by sharing the sub-dimension with another person, a decision I would soon come to regret. But I was outside of time, and the loan would not accrue interest until I finished the book, which if it was good enough, would cover the loan's amount, and I'd be out of debt and able to make a living as a writer.

And if it wasn't good enough, I would simply stay here until I made it good enough. I was in a place where time moved infinitesimally slower than time in the real world. Life extension drugs—included in my purchase—could reset me to my current age if I felt the need to spend lifetimes here. This house was, or at least should have been, a paradise.

Which was why it was confusing to me when I stepped outside and all that I could see was sand. The exception being the nearly identical house that sat a half dozen meters away. The images on Vogelfonte's marketing material always showed island paradises, or forested retreats, with famous writers relaxing with a pen and paper in their hands. I opted for the same, or at least similar, reality as the one Alexandra Hardy used to write her breakout masterpiece *The Moons of Her Eyes*. How she got something done in such a wasteland was a mystery to me, which I guess explained the lower package price despite the success associated with the location.

A weathered rocking chair sat on the porch and stared at the sandy horizon. It was unclear which was more uncomfortable, the hard wooden chair or the empty expanse of the horizon. Both were unsettling, so I decided that a hot and fresh meal would spark some inspiration. Preparing my own meal wouldn't be too hard. Humans have been doing it for generations, and it may be a good exercise in creativity.

I found some chicken thighs sealed tight in a bag in the refrigerator. Zucchini and broccoli were sitting in a drawer. I cut them into a variety of sizes, then gathered the most interesting sounding spices from the pantry. I planned to put together a stir fry. It seemed easy enough.

After all, the instructions were in the name. It was my favorite meal, so I had plenty of experience eating it. Cooking has never been my strong suit, never needed to be since there were plenty of units to prepare meals for me in all my apartments.

Quickly, I realized that this was not as simple as the automation robots made it seem. To make matters worse, the pan was flimsy, the spatula was bent, and the burner was just an electric coil. I'm not one who could appreciate high quality tools, but these surely weren't doing me any favors. Nonetheless, the food wound up on the plate, and the charred bits of meat made me confident it was done.

There was another serving still in the pan after filling a bowl to the brim, so I made a second bowl to take to the neighbor. Sticking a fork, chopsticks, and spoon into the rice, unsure of how they might like to eat it, I made my way across the few meters of sand with the piping hot bowls in my hands.

I heard someone shout "one minute," after hitting the doorbell with my elbow. Peeking through the windows, I noticed the layout was a mirror image of mine.

The door opened, and a man in a loosely tied bathrobe greeted me with hair so chaotic that I thought it'd jump off his scalp to attack me. "I'm your new neighbor," I said, introducing myself and offering him my lunch, likely his breakfast.

"Doug Smith," he replied, taking the stir fry out of my hand and gesturing me inside.

We sat at the small table, which was identical to the one in my house, and I took a bite of my meal. After removing the spare utensils out of his, Doug took a bite and immediately said, "This is utterly disgusting!"

I couldn't disagree with him. The flavor was nothing like the N-Ector versions of the meal, and despite burning the outside to a crisp, there were still pieces of meat that were raw on the inside. Nonetheless, I didn't appreciate his candor and continued to eat my portion out of spite. He cracked open a can of beans and warmed them on the stove as I started a conversation. "So what are you working on here?"

"I'm a musician," he said while stirring the beans in the bowl.

"What do you play?"

"Drums." He punctuated the statement by twirling his spoon between his fingers. It immediately clattered to the ground. Picking it up, he wiped the round end with his robe, placing a bean stain next to a dozen similar ones.

"That's exciting." And not knowing much about drums, or musicians in general, I said, "I'm a writer. I'm working on a novel."

He tasted the beans out of the bowl and decided they were warm enough and rejoined me at the table. "Don't you think there's enough of those already?"

"Which? Writers or novels?"

"Either," he said with a shrug. "Hasn't every story already been written? When I watched the net back home there were a dozen different space station noir shows. You can't tell me every one of those episodes is significantly different from the rest."

I didn't know how to respond at first. Formulaic dramas were nothing like the novel I planned to create. "Sure, there are similar themes and structures between stories, but our lives in the stars are far different from the mono-planet writers we inherited them from. And besides, haven't all the drums been beaten?"

"That's completely different," he said as he chewed a mouthful of beans. "Drums were made to be changed into different patterns, and there's value in me practicing existing music so that I can replicate it live. Not to mention drums are cool. Novels... that's just crap they make you read in school."

Fuming at the comparison, I could tell that his passion for the point would overcome any logic I tried to apply. I steered the conversation to his life before entering this sub-dimension. He was happy to share this information with me between bites of beans and eventually a mouth full of peaches plucked straight from their can.

As I scraped out the last bit of stir fry from the dish, a limp piece of zucchini, Doug said, "You know you don't have to mess with cooking that stuff." It was followed by an insufferable slurping sound as he drank the juice from the peach can. "Just eat the canned stuff; you only need to eat to keep your energy up."

"I mostly did it to give cooking a try."

"Well, I hope you're a better writer than a chef, otherwise you'll be here until the place folds in on itself."

"That's a thing that can happen?" I asked, concerned and trying to figure out if it was mentioned on one of the forms I signed after a quick skim.

He gave a hearty chuckle and said, "No, it's a turn of phrase. My turn of phrase. But if you want to use it you can."

I politely kept to myself the opinion that his phrase wasn't suited for any work of fiction or non-fiction I'd ever write. I soon worked my way out of the conversation by saying that I needed to get to writing before the day was over, and I wished him luck with his drum practice.

***

Sitting at the desk, I followed some printed instructions and eventually got the hang of using the typewriter. It was nearly as finicky as a word processor. I would align the paper exactly where I wanted the strikers to land, begin to type out the title of the novel, and it would somehow not be centered. After going through a dozen pieces of paper, I finally had the title "Giants Among Us" centered perfectly with my name underneath it. Rolling in a new blank piece of paper, everything was ready to begin my manuscript.

Doug had been so wildly lost on the subject of how creative writing could be. I had dozens of more options than he had drums, and I could combine each one to make countless words, then those made countless sentences, and then countless stories. Sure, stories shared some patterns and themes across the ages, and yes, space station noirs on the net could be repetitive. But this novel I had planned—a beautiful story about a fortune teller knowing her future husband was going to die of a brain disease then falling in love with him anyway—was like nothing else I'd ever read.

I looked over the keys, unsure of which letter to use first. The opening line had to be perfect, jaw-dropping, and gripping. I knew it had to give the reader enough to get into the story without disclosing everything. I wondered if I should start with the character's name, and I tried to find one that would suit her. Then I decided to write it in first person which settled that... for now. Since she was a fortune teller, I considered starting with a vision of the future, or maybe a flashback. As I worked to make the timeline come together in my head, something grabbed my stomach.

There should be medicine in the house to reduce my anxiety. My stomach began turning inside out, and I rushed to the bathroom, realizing that this wasn't the result of my anxiety.

Clutching the edges of the toilet, I ejected my lunch into the bowl. Saying that something in it didn't agree with me was an understatement. I kept retching even after I felt like I didn't have anything left inside me. Finally, I laid on the bathroom floor, defeated. I felt awful, and as soon as I could make it to bed, I vowed I'd lay there until my strength returned. No more writing would get done today.

I crawled into bed. The springs and metal posts creaked against each other. The mattress was unremarkable. Good enough to get a night's sleep but no zero-g sleep system. I groaned and wrestled with my stomach, which was now unhappy about something new despite being emptied. I didn't think I would ever fall asleep, but I must have because Doug's drum practice startled me awake.

I squinted at the clock. Its confusing arms gestured at two and twelve. I rolled over and found a pillow to cover my ears, hoping that Doug would only practice for a few minutes before going to bed. The pillow did little to help, and the drums continued for what felt like hours. By the time he finished, the morning light was creeping in through the window curtains.

I cannot sleep with a single ray of light in my room. I've always had artificial windows in my space station apartments, ones I could turn on and off at my whim. And the blinds of this house were doing little more than keeping prying eyes out. The light would only worsen as the morning dragged on, so I gave up and stumbled downstairs.

I milled around the house for the rest of the morning, trying baked beans I had to bake again, and refried beans which didn't benefit from a second frying. The canned fruits lacked the crispness of ones grown in the hydroponic farms. That, combined with my experience last night, made me hate just about everything I tasted.

Exhausted, I tried reading some of the books that were on the shelf. Unfortunately, the ones I'd read before didn't excite me, and the ones that were new to me didn't pull me in quick enough. Tired of trying to distract myself and hopeless that I'd get back to sleep, I sat down at the typewriter.

I typed the letter "I" on the first page, hoping it would inspire me. After all, I'd unintentionally read a dozen opening lines in an attempt to find something interesting to read. The rest of the words for the hook came to me, and I began to type the sentence out.

Every third letter typed, the machine replied with an unsettling scraping sound. I slowly typed the line's subsequent letters, watching the strikers swing up from where they rested, trying to find where the sound came from. It was unbearable to listen to, and if I were to write tens of thousands of words on this thing, it would be torture. I stopped mid-sentence and rummaged through the desk drawers to find something that might keep the thing from scraping. The drawers were void of any oil or tools, and I began pushing pens into the machine to see if I could realign its parts. A few characters later, I'd forgotten how I'd worded the rest of the sentence in my head. I let out a frustrated cry and went downstairs to keep myself from throwing the cursed thing out the window.

Pacing back and forth between the living room and dining room, I noticed a new sound that also seemed incessant. It was coming from the kitchen, and I moved around like a cat to see if I could hunt down the source of the noise. The culprit was soon apparent. The refrigerator made a constant whirring sound I hadn't noticed yesterday. Living on space stations, I'd grown accustomed to background hums and mechanical vibration. But I'd paid a good sum of money to live in this house in peace and quiet. And this refrigerator was making a sound I couldn't ignore.

Searching the house, I found a small bag of tools. I am no mechanic. I barely know where the ship dock is in any given station I've lived on. I pass through it when traveling and then forget its location until I need to leave. Any issue I've ever found in my living quarters required me to contact a licensed professional. Otherwise, I was likely to put a hole in something I wasn't supposed to and space myself and potentially everyone else on the station. Here, I didn't have that restraint. So, I began disassembling the refrigerator to stop the sound.

I twisted what I could, having a hard time finding the right tool, assuming it existed, and it was in the small tool bag. I fiddled with this project for a while, much longer than I tried my hand at cooking. Nonetheless, I enjoyed working on something and understood how some people could find a job like this rewarding. I began imagining the various mechanic characters I might work into my novel, trying to diverge from determined not to use the awful cliches. Finally, I wiggled a bit of the fridge's wiring that must have been out of place, and it silenced the machine.

My casual button-up shirt was covered in sweat. Walking around the house, I searched for a cool spot. I found a vent that was supposed to be sending fresh air into the house. However, it wasn't doing a great job. The afternoon sun had beaten its way into this place, and my air conditioning was unable to defend against it. I made a mental note to myself to use my newfound mechanic skills to work on that next.

I sat on the couch, exhausted, but the cloth seemed to absorb my sweat, keeping me from cooling down, so I migrated to a stiff kitchen chair. Unfortunately, it was near the sunniest window in the house. I finally lay down on the rough hardwood floor, and the cool air that sat on the floor helped me regulate my body temperature.

The refrigerator no longer hummed, and when my strength returned, I pushed it into place, removing a crispy green apple from the contraption. Exhausted from the lack of sleep and the amount of work I'd put into today, I sat on the porch now that the sun was making its way behind the horizon.

Rocking back and forth in the primitive wooden chair, I looked over to Doug's house and saw he was doing something similar. He had a beer in one hand and was playing some music through an old-style speaker system. I was glad the music didn't reach much past his porch since it was the raucous and chaotic rock 'n roll that every station's dive felt the need to play. I considered visiting him on his porch, but the conversation we'd shared last time was memorable in all the wrong ways. The day had been quiet, and I wondered if he'd been as uninspired as me today. Surely the middle of the night practice sessions weren't regular occurrences.

\*\*\*

Doug might as well be using my head for a drum. His music crashed through my ears all morning. Pillows and covers did little to drown out the noise. It'd been a week of incessant 2:00 AM drum practice leaving me hopelessly exhausted. I'd done little to no writing since arriving at this house. As consolation for putting up with his racket, I climbed out of bed for some ice cream.

For the past few days, the kitchen had a distinct odor. I always knew my cleaning wasn't up to par with the housekeeper bots installed in modern apartments, but the room was practically spotless. I opened the fridge, and a pungent smell slapped me in the face.

I quickly closed the door, but it was too late. For the past week, I begrudgingly followed Doug's advice and focused on eating canned food, as awful as it was. And since the refrigerator wasn't making a racket, I'd ignored it. Holding my nose and inspecting it further, I realized the box wasn't cold like it should've been. All the food was rancid, and the contents would only be valuable to biologists interested in studying the new species of mold inhabiting it.

Suited up in thick rubber gloves and a kitchen apron, I carried as much as I could to the house's recycler to be transported to some other sub-dimension or out of existence altogether. I didn't care as long as the smell wasn't abusing my nose.

I wrote a letter on Voglefonte-branded stationery, requesting more refrigerated food, and dropped it in the old-fashioned mailbox. The folks in charge of my experience would soon generate more food into my fridge. Before that happened, I needed to repair the thing. I undid my wiring repair until the thing began to make a racket again. I finished around the time Doug wrapped up his practicing. The silence I desired seemed to always evade me.

Sitting on the couch in an oversized shirt and loose shorts, I listened to the constant humming of the fridge. It was less erratic than Doug's performance but no more enjoyable. I wondered what the neighbor was doing, and I'm ashamed to admit that I went upstairs to peek out my window to see if I could see any movement in his house.

The curtains of his window were wide open. Doug lay passed out on his bed in nothing more than his underwear, unafflicted with the light sensitivity problem I was cursed with. Embarrassed to have viewed such a private moment, I closed my window curtain and went to the office to write.

The words came to me slowly, if at all, just like every other morning Doug's drumming woke me up. Staring at the typewriter, I thought of how I could bring up rescheduling his practice time, instead of what my characters might be doing. The most confrontational thing I'd done was write a politely worded message to a coworker, and I did not think that approach would go far with Doug.

I am not one to knock on my neighbor's door while they're sleeping, studying, or practicing. Nor would I bother them at night. Doug's schedule meant that I'd have to violate at least one of those things, which I would never appreciate someone doing to me. And so, I kept to my own house, hoping that Doug would soon master the drums so that I could begin writing my novel.

That delusion worked for a while, until I had to go over to Doug's house for his own safety.

\*\*\*

I woke up naturally at about a quarter to two, and I rolled over to go back to sleep. Knowing that drum practice was imminent kept me up. When silence still lingered in the house at a quarter to three, I knew something was wrong with Doug.

We are not simulated in these sub-dimensions. It's not some clunky virtual reality where your body is still in another world and your perception is the only thing that's moved. The Vogelfonte conglomerate moves our body here, and if we die here, we die in real life. I was confident in this fact above all other facts because I'd signed copious documents acknowledging that I was aware of it.

Meaning if Doug was in trouble, it was my responsibility as his neighbor to make sure that he was removed from this world before anything fatal happened. I would expect Doug, and everyone I'd ever shared a space station with, to do the same for me. Because despite all the life-extending drugs humanity has, we've yet to recombine bodies with their consciousness.

I lurked into his house. The front door was open. After all, I was the only person who could rob his stockpile of beans, and his supply matched mine.

There was no one on the first floor, so I proceeded to the second floor. His stairs creaked as much as mine did. Calling out for Doug didn't return any acknowledgment, and so I continued into the bedroom. The bed was a mess, and clothes were piled high on the floor. The dresser, bedside table, and even the bed's headboard had kitchen pots and empty cans littered across them. A beat cop from a space station noir might classify this as a sign of a struggle, but I suspected it was Doug's way of life.

Crossing the hall to his study, I cracked the door open, unsure of what I would find, and I hoped Doug was conscious or at least his organs were still working. I peeked through the slit of the door. At first, the sight in front of me confused me, but once I gathered what was going on, I stumbled away in desperation.

Doug sat on a round stool surrounded by drums and cymbals of various sizes. Each drum had a hole or split in the taught plastic cover. None of them made a sound as he whacked his stick against it. Despite the damaged equipment, he still swung his sticks wildly through the air, hitting the drums despite their mute response. The cymbals lay on the ground, their broken stands leaning against the wall. Despite this, he still beat his sticks onto the site where the cymbals would have perched. Doug, not exactly humanity's finest specimen, was completely mad. And I made the mistake of intruding into his den.

As I backed away, I tripped on a loose pan. I fell to the ground with a loud clatter. Doug swiveled around in his stool and saw me laying on the ground.

"I was trying really hard to ignore you," he groaned, "but you don't make it easy. Did you come to see why there was no ballad tonight?" His mouth was crooked with a smile that sent a chill down my spine.

"I... I just... I just wanted to make sure you were okay."

Doug cackled. "Right as rain."

"Your drums don't work," I pointed out. Mostly to make sure I was still the sane one in this interaction.

He shrugged and twirled a drumstick between his fingers with more success than he'd had with the spoon. "They work as well as they ever have," he assured me.

Glad that he'd confirmed my sanity, I said,. "They're all busted and not making noise."

"Oh," he said as if I'd just explained the answer to a riddle. "The sticks still work. And I've got a dozen more of these."

"But you're not making a sound," I protested, despite being glad for the silence.

"I'm not here to make sound," he said in a tone I hadn't heard since graduating school. "I'm here to swing sticks." He presented the sticks to me, found a crack in one, and snapped it in half, tossing it onto a pile of similar sticks. "Now, if you don't mind, I am going to get back to work. After all, I don't interrupt you while you're writing."

I began to protest, but he swept his fingers at me in a gesture to get going. I backed out politely, closing the door behind me. As I walked down the stairs, I heard him call out, "Don't worry, I'll order new drumheads in the morning, so the performances will return tomorrow."

I don't know if my groan reached back up the stairs, and I don't think Doug would have cared if it had.

Frustrated by the absurdity of the night, I lay in bed, hoping the silence would help me to sleep. But no, I was like an acclimated third shift worker unable to stay awake during the day cycle. I gave up sooner than expected and dragged myself across the hall into my office.

Sitting in front of the typewriter, I began to swing my sticks. My fingers picked keys at random, adding ink to the page. Soon, I reached the end of the page, so I rolled it back to the first line and typed over the previous characters.

I kept punching keys, looking forward to the scraping that happened to every third key—resetting the page to the header before it fell out the back. I used up all the ribbon's ink and watched the strikers stamp the black page with faint imprints of the letters. Doug's ridiculous practice had cursed me with wakefulness. I might as well play along with the same absurd disinterest he had of the outcome.

The sun eventually rose and beat through the window curtains. Daylight delivered some practicality, or as much as there was to be had here. I took the marred and stained paper out of the typewriter and pinned it on the wall.

I replaced the ribbon and rolled a fresh piece of paper into the machine. I knew how to swing my sticks without losing focus, so I began writing a story. Not one where the plot was undiscovered and characters had yet to receive names. I typed out a story I knew by heart because I'd just lived it. And it began with a house just this side of falling apart.

The story I wrote that day was garbage, and it's been garbage the past three times I've written it. One day, it might be decent enough to let someone read, but for now, I merely type the story out, stack the page, and load in the next blank one. After a few more sentences, I'll sit on the porch and look out to the sandy horizon of this wasteland. I'll go about my day, breaking or fixing things as needed, and then get to bed early so I can be well-rested.

Tomorrow will begin as it always does, with a racket early in the morning, reminding me to swing my sticks.

# Muck and Miscreants

Published August 5, 2022 -
StepIntoTheRoad.com

I remember wading through the streets with muck on my boots and neon lights buzzing in my ears. Hordes of people flowed past me as if they were fish in the stream, merely following the current while I defied them and their conventions. After what I'd done, it was no shock that I felt like a heretic. I wore the collar of my stained brown trench coat high to hide the scars, not that anyone in the street was interested in anything other than getting home with their dinner, taking off their dirty shoes, and resting before another day struck them. I was interested in much the same, but my prospects were looking worse by the minute.

The smell of the sea and fishmonger's wares still pummeled my nostrils, filling my mind with their pungency. The random cries of products for sale in the local's bastardized dialect of Common Tongue still startled me since I had no way to filter the noise out. I wanted nothing more than to be off the street and get some quiet for my new senses.

I turned down a short alley and knocked on the scrap metal door, a thin piece of corrugated metal that time and sea air ate away at the edges. Its hinges squeaked as the innkeeper peaked through the slit she'd made. "You want what?" she asked.

I kept my head down and angled my body, so only my good eye faced her. "Room for the night, please." Mixing the order of my words to try to sound like a citizen of the city would only confuse both of us. "I have credits," I added as she looked at me dubiously.

"No trouble," she said.

At first, my heart fluttered with hope. When she didn't open the door any further, I slowly realized I'd missed a cue. My old implants would have informed me that this was a question, not a statement. Her irritated voice repeating the message with squinted eyes prodded me to respond.

"No, I'm no trouble. I have credits." I gave her my best smile. The left side of my mouth twisted from where they removed the subvocalizer.

"No manticores!" The squeak of the door closing was short, and the staccato of the latch punctuated her statement.

Despite having the same natural cognition as everyone else here, I was not welcome. The scales had fallen from my eyes, and the overlay text and video had gone with them. I was far from a manticore now but still as despised as a tax collector.

However, it was the right thing for her to do. Giving me a bed could ruin her reputation in the city or, worse, pit her against the conglomerate that ruled this planet. The same conglomerate that fired me for reporting accurate census data to the Central System.

That action had gone against the conglomerate's best interest. Soon a minister judge would be out to evaluate and hopefully improve the living conditions of these citizens, assuming my former colleagues didn't misreport other numbers first.

They charged me with misallocation of equipment, citing that I'd overordered meal rations. An act that everyone did at some point. On a station with standard rations, this could lead to the starvation of the crew. However, unlike the city around me, our station was overflowing with meals, equipment, and space.

I lost my position and implants, leaving me with the biological standards and scars on half my face. My meat memory is no computer and is flawed with inaccuracies and gaps. But I remember this moment at the inn door better than the painful uninstallation surgery or the slap of the fish breeze at the landing shuttle's doorway.

I was shocked that my unenhanced ears noticed the door squeaking back open. A young boy's face peaked out. "Two down doors and an alleyway away. They take your credits and face."

The innkeeper angrily shouted at him, and he slinked away, latching the door closed.

I hoped his punishment was less than mine. Thanks to the little miscreant boy, my prospects of a quiet bed had improved.

# The Majesties Watch Over You

Published January 7, 2022 -
StepIntoTheRoad.com

C raning your neck out, you can see flecks of light in the thin gap between your building and the one next to you. The towers reach into the darkness above and below. Days earlier, you accidentally broke the window while exercising. Since then, you've come home every night to stare up at the Majesties and their beauty.

You have to stick your head out to see them, and it's a long way down, but their twinkle locks your gaze upward. The education videos they showed you as a kid never mentioned their existence. It didn't explain the light blue canvas that replaces them in the morning either. The entertainment videos, which you've replaced with the Majesties, don't mention anything like it.

Before you could put your head out, the window only showed the blank bricks of the opposing building. The building is so close you could almost reach out and touch it. But your focus is on the Majesties and their slow journey across the gap.

If your supervisor inspected your room and saw the white bed sheet hanging like a curtain and what it hid, she would fine you for the malcompliance and demote you three positions back on the conveyor belt that you've spent countless pay cycles working your way up. But your chest twists in protest every time you imagine betraying the Majesties.

Above you, a new pinprick of light appears. It begins its voyage across the finger-width gap. There are only a few hundred Majesties above you, and if you focus, you could tally them all. Unfortunately, they disappear from your view and behind the opposing building.

Quickly, a Majesty flicks across the gap, leaving a streak of light behind as it vanishes. Your gaze returns to the previous one as it moves slowly above you.

Your stomach groans, and your eyelids feel heavy. You should be unfolding your bed from the wall of the small apartment right now. The ration you received from your work on the assembly line today grew cold hours ago.

But the Majesty you're watching is only a few hair lengths away from hiding behind the blackness of your neighboring building. You fight to keep your eyes open as it leaves your line of sight.

You crane your head out to see if you can get one last glimpse of it before it disappears for good. This is the most you've ever left the building. It's been a wonderful evening with these beauties, and you can't bear its ending.

Holding the windowsill, you lean out to prolong your view. Greedy for a final peek, you stretch your chest out further.

Your feet slip. Your grip isn't as tight as it should be. The majority of your body was hanging out the window. It drags the minority out to join it. There's no longer anything solid around you. Your guts feel like they're lurching from your stomach.

The pulling feeling is tenfold mightier than the elevators that take you to and from the assembly lines. Your shoulder scratches a wall on one side, and you tumble to hit the opposite building. It feels like someone's placed an orbital sander against your shoulder. But you look up and see the comforting Majesties shining down on you.

The few hundred watch you fall just as you watched them cross the gap. Your body reconnects with something solid, and the lurching sensation stops. The Majesties watch over you, alone in the alley between the buildings, as you cross over into the darkness.

# Path of the Bearers

Published September 1, 2022 - Path of the
Bearers and Other Stories

A lvin climbed over the back of the couch as he headed for the
door.

"How many times have I told you not to do that?" Mom handed
him his sandals.

Alvin didn't answer; he could tell by her tone it wasn't a real question. He strapped his sandals, imagining they were the big, powered
boots he was about to be wearing. After sliding the corrugated metal
door open, he skipped down the stairs. Mom let out a sigh and a call
after him, but he was already at the ground floor and ready to punch
in the code to exit the apartment complex. He still wasn't allowed past
it without one of his mothers, but today he'd get to go further than
he'd ever gone before.

The apartment complex was in the old style: sturdy metal walls
with atmosphere locks in case of emergency. The living quarters inside
were newer and made of scavenged hardware to increase the number
of rooms, and families, the building could hold. The new style wasn't
as sturdy, and he couldn't climb on the walls, even though there were
so many good footholds.

When Mom made it to the bottom of the stairs, he punched in the code as quickly as possible. He mistyped the five to be a four, and the door wouldn't let him out. By the time he retyped it, she was standing behind him. The door opened with a swish, and he looked out at the bustling streets of Balteras.

The dome overhead shimmered as power flowed through it. Large buildings in the smooth and shiny metal of the old style sat like boulders in the street. Newer buildings, mostly shops and restaurants, were littered between them. The newest buildings used wood, barrels, and canvas sheets to make their walls and furniture. They had to use anything the scouts brought back. Groups of people walked along the streets, some laughing, others with their heads down, trying to navigate the river of people.

Alvin headed toward the dome's edge, but Mom called after him.

"We're going out today to see the Bearers," he reminded her. Mama always joked that she might accidentally forget his birthday, but Mom would never forget something so important.

"First we have to go to Otler park."

Alvin groaned as his shoulders deflated. This wasn't supposed to be another day at the park. This was his birthday, his fourteenth birthday, and he was supposed to go see the path of the Bearers.

"We'll head out soon, but we have to go there first."

Alvin loved the jungle gyms of Otler park. He would stand above them and felt like he was on the top of the Balteras dome, or at least he was taller than both of his mothers. The playsets seemed to be shrinking though because now he could reach the monkey bars with a small jump and didn't need much more than the bottom step of the stairs to be taller than Mom. Plus, his other friends, even the ones who hadn't seen the Bearers, were bored of it. They wanted to play Titan Clash, a trading card game that Alvin could never learn all the rules to.

Whenever they got engrossed in that, he pulled out his sampler and recorded the battle sounds they made or other sounds in Balteras.

Alvin realized something and ran back to Mom. "I forgot my sampler!" They'd have to go back to the apartment for it. He didn't want to miss the opportunity to record the sounds from outside the dome for the first time.

Mom pulled the device out of her pocket, the old-fashioned microphone cord wrapped around the device. "You'll have to be careful with this. Mama will be upset if you lose it."

"I know. I'll be careful." Mama had found the device on a scouting mission and brought it back for him. There weren't many pieces of equipment like it, and a tinkerer had to do special work to get it to communicate with their family's terminal so Alvin could make music with the audio samples he recorded during the day.

They arrived at the center of Otler park, at the statue of William Otler. It was Alvin's least favorite part of the park because it was the one thing there he wasn't allowed to climb. A small fence surrounded the statue and the Eark it held. He couldn't climb it because the Eark powered the whole dome of Balteras. The dome was necessary—as Alvin had learned in every history class he ever sat through—to keep the air in and the monsters of their planet, Thachit, out. The Eark was transported by the Bearers from Paltov, the original city, to Balteras.

"Why do you think we started here?" Mom sounded like a teacher, and Alvin wanted to get this over with as soon as possible.

The Eark glowed purple in the center with sparks of lapis flowing up into the sky and creating dark streaks on the city's dome. A metal cage rotated around the purple core, ignoring gravity and drifting at its own leisure. A shallow dome like a satellite dish rested on the statue's shoulders, and Alvin knew it was key to keeping the Eark in place.

"I don't know," Alvin replied.

The Eark gave off a faint buzzing he'd tried to capture a few times, but his microphone wasn't sensitive enough.

His mother gave him a look that encouraged him to try harder. He didn't want to get the journey outside the dome taken away.

"Because Otler was the last of the Bearers."

"And enabled the Eark and city of Balteras to continue on," his mother continued. "What does the sign under Otler say?"

The statue wasn't really a statue, but the platform it was on had been added after Otler's suit took the kneeling stance, holding the Eark on his shoulder and hands. The shallow dish was still wired into his suit, although power had left the suit generations ago when Balteras was founded.

Alvin read the inscription. "If I have seen further, it is by standing on the shoulders of giants." He squinted at the next word. "Anony..." He wrinkled his eyebrows; this was one of those dumb words that he didn't know.

"Anonymous," his mother finished. "Do you know why it's there?"

"Because the Eark went from shoulder to shoulder of the Bearers."

"Very good," she said, "Do you want to play before we head out?"

Alvin shook his head and started down the road that led to the dome's edge. He was ready to head out on the day's adventure.

***

The third Bearer looked the same as the first two. It was kneeling like Otler, but their arms were stretched out to pass the Eark to the next Bearer, the one they'd looked at ten or fifteen minutes ago.

A small sign was posted in front of the statue, and Mom read it. Alvin was more interested in the suit the bearer was wearing. It was the same model his mom wore, just covered in sand and dried-out tubing.

Alvin's suit was less advanced and lacked some features like extended comms and an electric rifle. The hydraulic muscles were less powerful since he was smaller. The old man who fitted him in the suit kept calling it a child's suit, and Alvin didn't appreciate this since he was fourteen and leaving the dome. But he figured once you had some gray hairs in your beard like him, everyone looked like a kid to you.

The old man was nice enough to strap the sampler to the suit's forearm. Alvin had already captured the sound of wind in the microphone. But outside the dome was a quiet desert, and the suits they visited were silent, shut down years ago once the Eark was passed from their possession.

"How'd they get the person out after they placed the Eark?" Alvin asked his mother. School had taught him about what the Bearers did and how his ancestors continued to lead the city of Balteras. But he never learned the details of what the Bearers did after they moved the Eark.

"They didn't remove them," his mom replied.

"They couldn't stay in there," Alvin explained to his mother. "The filters would fail, and there'd be no way for them to eat or breathe or use the bathroom." He was restating all the things the old man at the gate had told them about why it was important to monitor the suit's power.

"The suit is also heavy," his mother continued in her teaching voice, "they wouldn't be able to move it on their own; the suit's muscles are the only thing that allow us to move."

"So, they are stuck in there forever?"

"That's why the Bearers are so important. Because they used all their suits' power to move the Eark away from Paltov to where we are today."

Alvin looked at the suit around him instead of through the face-plate. The man taught him how to use it as an extension of his body, and it was neat being able to move quickly, jump high, and set it into a seated position, so you could use it like a chair. But thinking about what his mother said, he could feel that the suit was only a centimeter away from his body, and if it quit working, his range of motion would go from super human to nothing. He checked his battery power; it was ninety percent charged. Surely it would take him to the end of the path.

"What if we don't make it to the end of the path with our battery?" he asked.

"Remember, Mr. Adams said there was a charging station in the original city."

"Oh yeah, right." Alvin did remember the old man saying that. The man had said a lot of stuff while Alvin was getting into the suit, and he wondered how much of it was this important.

As they traveled across the desert, his mother stopped at every Bear-er they passed. He didn't like stopping, especially because the signs were all the same except for the bearer's name, and it always made him aware of the suit so uncomfortably close to his skin.

But after leaving the Bearers, Alvin wasn't bothered by the dread the suit held. He liked to bound ahead of Mom, the suit's strength making him faster than he ever was on the city's streets. He enjoyed doing this until he saw a kneeling Bearer on the horizon, and he'd walked up to it slowly, which was still quicker than he could ever run without the suit.

About midway between two Bearers Alvin found an amazing rock formation. It looked like a noodle dish Mama made, and it was larger than any jungle gym he'd ever explored. He darted toward it, his hydraulically reinforced legs carrying him there faster than expected.

"Alvin, don't play on that," Mom called out through the radio.

He ignored her and grabbed onto the rock face with his thick armored gloves. The rock crumbling under his grip made a neat sound, so he turned on his sampler.

His mother called out again; she was always saying something or another about not climbing things, but he was an adult now, he was in a hydraulic suit, and nothing could hurt him. His boots were strong and could kick through the face of the rock to make footholds. In no time, he was standing on top of the structure, surveying the world around him.

Thachit was a barren planet. Some teachers explained that it was only the area they lived in that was barren, and old satellite images showed forests, oceans, and mountains, but Balteras wasn't set up there. There were dangerous creatures in those areas that made it unrealistic to set up the Eark. The sandy desert was safer than anywhere else, especially once the Eark was moved away from the forest's edge where the original city sat.

"Alvin, get down from there," his mother radioed. He could see her running up to the formation.

He jumped from one of the noodles to another, getting higher and higher on the structure. His boots crunched the rock underneath him, and he hoped his sampler was picking things up as well as his suit's microphone.

"That's a xantur hive," she continued.

With that, Alvin froze, and he wanted to jump down from the structure. But he'd made it too high, and he didn't know if the suit could survive the jump.

Of course, this was a hive; they'd shown him pictures in school. He never remembered important things like this. There was something else important that he knew he wasn't remembering. He was so silly for kicking and stomping on it. There would probably be a swarm of the ferocious creatures on him in no time.

"It's okay, Alvin," his mom said, her electric rifle now in her hands. "Just carefully climb down. You're a good climber. You can do it."

He looked down, and there was a noodle running under him; he could jump there and then to the ground. Pushing off the platform with his strong boots, he flew through the air. He was on track to land on the lower structure. He'd be next to his mom in no time. His mom was shouting something across the radio, but his chest was light with excitement from the fall. It was like jumping off a swing set.

His feet landed on the lower structure for a moment. And as he fell through it, he remembered the important thing they'd taught him about the hives. The structures were hollow. The heavy suit broke through the tube's wall, and he was inside the xantur hive. The darkness triggered the suit's headlights to turn on, but he still couldn't see much because the xantur beasts had coated the inside of the tunnel with slime. He slid down the tunnel like a slide, calling out to his mom on the radio. He flailed his arms, trying to grab something, but despite his super strength, everything was too slick to grasp.

He felt nauseous from the drops and turns the tunnel made; he was worried he'd vomit and not be able to see out of the helmet's window. Then the sliding stopped. He hadn't heard from his mother on the radio since his fall into the tunnel. There was something that the old man said to do when he was in a bad situation.

Curled up in a ball, stationary on the floor of a room, the suit had protected him. It would continue to protect him even after it ran out of power and stood as still as a statue. The realization brought him little comfort. He wanted to cry but knew it would make a mess in the suit.

There were other ways the suit could protect him. It didn't have an electric gun, but the old man said it could signal for help. He found the switch; it was bright red and covered with a protective latch. He flipped it. He was relieved that his mother would soon receive the signal and come to get him from wherever he was.

He sat in a dark cave, sitting up in his suit but unable to stand because it was still slick around him. Slime dripped from tubes in the ceiling and walls. It covered the ground and the feet of his suit. He must have slid through one of the many tunnels in the wall.

He was under the ground in a xantur hive. Without any weapons or help. The signal might not even get through the ground around him. He'd be stuck in this cave forever, inside the suit forever. Just like the Bearers. Except he wasn't doing something great, he wasn't carrying an ancient piece of technology that kept an entire city of people safe. He was a rambunctious kid, just like his moms always said. He couldn't hold back the tears anymore; he cried, just like when he was a kid and scraped his knee climbing on new construction. Mama always said it was okay to cry, and so he did. He let loose. And immediately was reminded of the shell he was trapped in.

He couldn't wipe away his tears while inside the exo-suit. He couldn't move more than a centimeter without the exo-suit responding to his movements. But whenever it ran out of power, it'd quit responding, and he'd be trapped even more. He cried more, and soon, the inside of the suit was covered with as much slime as the outside.

Alvin stopped crying when his suit moved in the pool of slime. Startled, he turned to see that a xantur was standing near him. He tried to get up but failed again, the room around him too slick to get a foothold in. The curious xantur scurried away, comfortable moving in the slime. Alvin saw it took refuge in a pack of a dozen other xanturs cluttered near an opening in the wall.

Scared of the beasts, he shouted all the adult words he knew. The words the older kids used on the playground and that teachers didn't let him say in school. The xantur shouted back, but not in any words he understood.

The two-legged creatures had small arms near their face. The arms didn't bend in the middle like human arms. They were more like horns that swung open and shut. The word mandible came to mind; it was a word his teacher used when describing them, and he hated that his mind could remember things now but not earlier in the day.

The xantur continued making sounds, swinging their mandibles open and shut, making a mix between the song of a flute and the cry of a baby. Scared by the loud chorus of bugs, Alvin curled into a ball again. Occasionally, a xantur approached, and he swung his arm wild to keep them away. The first few times the approaching xantur backed away. When they approached a couple at the same time, he swung out, and two grabbed his arm in their mandibles.

He flailed his other arm and his legs at the beasts, but soon, pairs approached and grabbed those, too. Alvin was terrified they'd pull his limbs off despite the suit's tight seals. There were dozens of the bugs now. And despite his super muscles, he couldn't pull his arms or legs out of their mouths. The suit was bolted together tightly, but they had the numbers and strong back feet. They'd crack into it eventually if they wanted.

Scared of what was to come, he cried out for help as the xanturs carried him down a tunnel. The fine claws of their feet seemed to slip past the slime and grip into the rock of the tunnel. Every once in a while, the tunnel would narrow enough that the xantur would lose their grip, and Alvin flailed his arm to keep them back. But they always kept his other limbs held tight. He watched the waist-high creatures get his arm back under control and continue to pull him through the tunnel.

His suit went wild every once in a while as the creatures hit the controls on his forearm. His headlights flashed on and off depending on how they held him, and multiple times the suit began a diagnostic run only to be cut off by some other manual command the bugs input. He could hear them making various sounds to each other like old jazz musicians that could change rhythm and tempo on the fly. The creatures were terrifyingly alien, and if this is what Thachit held under the surface, then he didn't want to know what the forest and oceans held.

After being carried by the creatures for some time, it stopped. They'd switched off his light at this point by jostling him through the tunnels, but the bugs seemed to still know where they were going. They still sat in a tunnel, and Alvin heard scratching. He wondered if they were beginning to try to cut through his suit.

Suddenly, his light turned on. It was brighter than anything his suit could produce. He was moving again, and they were shoving him out of the tunnel. He was being pushed toward the bright light, and soon, he was dropped on his back, staring up at the sun. He stood up, ready to run away from the beasts as they let go, but he saw they beat him to it. Retreating into a noodle that rose from the ground, they began repairing the hole they'd ejected him from. They balled up slime with each other, using their mandibles, and patched a hole in their rock structure.

Adjusting the dials and switches of his suit, he made sure he was still sending a distress call to his mother or anyone that might be searching for him.

He realized something was missing from the arm of his suit. The sampler Mama had found for him must have fallen off while he was being transported through the tunnels. He was devastated and regretted ever bringing it on the trip.

His battery power was below half, and he didn't know where he was on Thachit. His mother's suit had a comms array that would locate him on the planet or at least relative to the Eark, but he was too weak to pick that signal up. He waited, drenched in slime, hoping his mother would arrive.

***

Looking up at the tunnel, he saw the hole wasn't patched all the way up. A small fist-sized hole still remained, and from it popped a small rock-like thing. It was covered in blue slime, much like him, and he watched the beasts patch up the last of the hole.

He rushed up to the debris and soon saw it was the sampler. A light was blinking, indicating that the memory was full, and he remembered he'd started recording back when he was on top of the world. While he waited for Mom to arrive, he listened to the sounds the xantur made in the hive. No longer surrounded by darkness, the creatures weren't as scary when he listened to them. He used the machine's buttons to bookmark sounds that were interesting to him so he could feature them in his music later.

\*\*\*

Eventually, Mom arrived, and they hugged as best they could in their exo-suits. He apologized profusely about climbing on the rock structure. She told him it was okay, and she helped him reattach the sampler to his arm. They headed back to the path of the Bearers.

When they eventually found a Bearer on the horizon, the way the suit faced pointed them toward Balteras. The sign said that this was the 7th Bearer of the Eark. Which meant they were close to Paltov.

"You don't have much further to go," Mom said.

"Can't we just go home?" Alvin didn't want to be out here anymore, and he didn't want to see any more dead people inside of exo-suits. He wanted to be at home with his moms on the comfortable couch, watching something on his terminal.

"It's too far back to the Eark." His mom sounded concerned, like when Mama was late back from a scouting mission. "We don't have enough battery power to get there."

Alvin checked his own suit. He didn't have much energy left.

His mom was explaining some calculations that he didn't understand, then she said, "You're going to have to go on to the charger in Paltov without me."

"No, I can't!" he protested.

"You have to," she said, and her tone was matter of fact, as if she was making him take a bath.

"I don't have the power to get there. You said it."

"I'm going to give you what I have left." She disconnected something from her suit and plugged it into his. Alvin watched his battery charge up just past halfway. His mother's battery capacity was bigger than his, and if she could only fill his suit up this much, then she must have used a lot of energy searching for him while he was gone.

"Just follow the Bearers," she said as she locked the armor into a seated position. "I'll be here when you get back."

"I can't go," he continued to complain, but his suit notified him that his mother's communication had gone offline. He was speaking, but she couldn't hear. Eventually, he gave up trying to convince his statue of a mother to change her mind and continued down the path of the bearers.

***

The battery's charge dropped by a few percentage points every time Alvin passed a Bearer. Each Bearer inside the frozen suit spent their energy carrying the heavy Eark as far as they could. Draining every last watt the battery had. Alvin could carry himself as far as they went with only a few percentage points of power. But it still took almost all the power he had to get to the end of the path.

He saw the city that sat at the end of the path on the horizon, taking up more of his field of view than any kneeling Bearer. It was an ancient city made of the most advanced metals humanity knew, according to his teachers. The buildings were in the old style, smooth rounded metal with no obvious joinery. They stood up to the beating that was Thachit's weather. The only visible damage was made by scouts looting metal from the walls and dragging anything that moved out of the storehouses. The buildings shone like a metal slide worn smooth by countless children sliding down it. Each one a small mound on the horizon like an ice cream treat spread across the horizon.

When he arrived at the city, the forest was nearly visible on the horizon. It looked like closely cropped hair. Older kids bragged about exploring it, but if it was half as bad as the xantur tunnels, he wanted to stay away. According to the old man that fitted him for his suit, the scout reports said this area was clear from beasts. Otherwise, the birthday adventure would be delayed.

Alvin stepped over the line that marked the old city's edge. It was still apparent after generations because it was a thick glass ring. The Eark's power made it a cloudy and imperfect glass, but it was large enough to be immovable by natural forces. If Balteras' dome ever went down, a similar ring would be visible. Alvin looked through the city for a cart and a charging station. The scouts had marked the buildings with arrows and acronyms, and he followed them through the city, not knowing what the letters represented. Each step in the suit took him further than he could go on the busy streets of Balteras, but too much wandering would lead to an empty battery.

Following a rounded corner through the city's street he heard the buzzing of the charging station before he saw it. A cart sat nearby, maybe left there by a scout like Mama. Excited, he started for the cart and station, but froze as soon as he noticed movement between the cart and the charger.

He should have seen it before. He should have approached slower or from another angle. Mom always said he had FTL vision. So focused on getting to a singular point he didn't see things around him. The beast stood up on its hind legs, its disproportionately long arms occasionally helping it stabilize as it walked toward Alvin.

The beast was a gartun, a forest predator, and one of the reasons Paltov was abandoned. Biologists classified it as ape-like although, much like the biologists, Alvin had only seen a few old pictures of apes. Unlike apes, the gartun had a long snout that came to a flat end with slits in it. The slits flared as it approached the cart, and Alvin felt trapped in his powerful suit, trying to think of how to escape the beast.

He ran out of time to think and plan when the beast rushed toward him. It lumbered down the street, using all four limbs to speed toward him. Alvin turned and ran, not caring about the battery life on his suit.

He knew running from a predator was bad; Mama had told him it a dozen times over dinner or whenever they watched old scary movies. He had to stand his ground or hide. But the gartun seemed as tall as the buildings around him, so standing his ground was not an option.

The bright spray paint that scouts used on buildings caught Alvin's attention. Some doors had been pulled off buildings, and when he spotted a door bent off its sliding guide, he dove inside the small opening. His suit scraped against the old metal, but he fit in. If he'd been any bigger, he wouldn't have fit. He turned, terrified the beast would lift the entire building up around him.

All he could hear in his suit's speakers was the gartun's sniffing. He looked at the opening he'd come through. It was covered in a shining liquid, and Alvin worried he'd busted a hydraulic tube. His suit didn't report a leak. Then the gartun did the strangest thing. Its tongues reached into the hole and flailed about.

Alvin backed away into a wall. The tongues were bigger than his arms. They covered the opening of the door, licking it clean. It was like the beast was licking a lollipop. The liquid wasn't hydraulic fluid but left-over slime from his excursion in the xantur caves. The beast had found him because he smelled like xanturs. And he doubted the gartun could tell the difference between his suit and a xantur carapace.

Stuck in the old building, Alvin knew he needed help. He could wait for a scout to come by, but that could be days, maybe less if he and his mom didn't return. He couldn't wait though, because his mom was stuck in the middle of the desert, unable to move and sitting prey for anything as scary as the gartun.

He was creative and smart. His moms and teachers had told him that plenty of times. He had to come up with a solution. It probably wouldn't be a solution like other kids would come up with—adults quit expecting that of him a long time ago—but he did enjoy solving problems. Problems like climbing up chaotic building walls or putting together music with the sounds his friends made.

There was nothing to climb in the smooth architecture of this old building. But he had a super-powered suit. He checked his wrist, scared for a moment, but the sampler was still there; he was grateful for that.

The sampler had xantur sounds on it. He was excited to make music with that when he got home. They had so many complex cries. The xantur had just ejected him from their homes. He didn't expect the gartun to do that though. But he was scared inside the xantur tunnel. Maybe the small xantur that first approached him was scared, too. But that xantur had reinforcements. Or at least did after he called out for them. The sound was like a flute and the cry of a baby. He remembered it clearly and had bookmarked it on his sampler to use later.

Maybe he could use it now. Lure the xantur here to help. They may not eject him out of the building, but they might be a distraction for the gartun. The gartun could eat his rightful prey, instead of Alvin.

He pressed the button that played back the xantur's call. The gartun immediately backed away from the door. He hoped that was a good sign, but then the beast started banging on the building. Alvin felt like he was trapped inside a drum.

The beating was incessant, and old furniture and tools that still lingered inside the building shook around him. He hoped that it would hold up because it was an old building but didn't know how powerful the gartun might be.

Then he heard a second cry; it was barely audible over the thuds that shook the building; it came from an air vent in the building. Alvin stacked some desks and chairs up, moving the furniture without an issue with his powerful suit and climbed to the vent.

A xantur sat waving its mandibles back and forth, repeating the sound coming from his wrist. He pulled the grate off the vent. When it came free, he fell back to the ground, but the suit protected him. A dozen xantur crawled into the room from the vent, having no problem clinging to the smooth walls of the metal building.

They surrounded him on the ground, repeating the call coming from his wrist. He didn't know what to do next. He hesitated to even get up since the xantur might perceive him as the threat now that they could see him.

The gartun's banging stopped. Its nose went to the door, sniffing, then it clawed at the opening with its large fingers, trying to poke a hole through the metal building. The xantur got louder and changed their cadence. If Alvin's sampler still had memory he'd start recording; it was crazier than any monster sounds his friends ever made.

More xantur filled in from the air vent, repeating the sound of the others. The bug-like creatures surrounded the door. The gartun sniffed it again, unable to stick a finger in. It began licking the opening like it had before.

The two arm-like tongues flailed around, but a xantur bit onto the tongue with its mandibles. The gartun made a squeal, and the xantur replied with a similar sound. Other xanturs latched onto the beast as it pulled its tongues out of the doorway. They were carried out the door, Alvin felt bad they were about to be eaten by the beast.

The xantur that didn't get a hold of the tongues filed out of the door. Alvin followed at a distance and watched as the xanturs on the ground began attacking the gartun's feet and legs. Grasping through the beast's wiry fur, they pinched it, and the gartun stepped away, trying to avoid the pinches.

Alvin snuck out the building and saw that the xanturs were still holding onto the tongues. Their strong back legs kept it from going inside the mouth by bracing against its flat nose and lips. The gartun stumbled away from the opening of the building, still trying to avoid the bites of the little pests. Its hands clawed at its face, trying to clean off its tongue.

As fascinating as the interaction was, Alvin's battery power was low, and he needed to get the cart back to Mom. He went back the way he came, the path obvious because of the large footmarks the gartun left in the sandy streets. He found the cart and drove it into the protective dome of the charging station. He wired himself up and waited for his suit to return to full power. In the distance, he could hear the gartun screaming in pain.

Alvin was frightened as his suit reached full charge because the gartun wandered down the street. He wondered if the beast might want revenge and what might have happened to the little xanturs. But the beast had large red welts all over its body, and it walked slowly on all four of its limbs, favoring one leg over the other. It passed by without even sniffing in Alvin's direction.

*** 

The cart was harder to drive than the video games he'd played with friends, but in the open desert of Thachit he had plenty of room for error. He soon found Mom on the path of the bearers, the sun beginning to dip under the horizon. He plugged her in, worried that something would be wrong with her despite the suit being hard and protective.

"Are you okay, Alvin?" she asked once her suit had enough power to communicate.

"I'm fine, but you'll never believe what happened." Alvin excitedly shared what happened as his mom's suit charged up. She couldn't have moved away from his story, but he also knew she didn't want to. Neither of his moms ever left him when he was sharing a story from the playground, and this was no different.

When Mom's suit was charged, she drove the cart back home. She kept saying that she was so glad he was okay, and he found it annoyingly repetitive. They got to Balteras after dark, and in the receiving room where they would take off their suits, Mama was waiting, a worried look on her face.

"Mama, I have a recording to show you!" Alvin said as she helped him out of the exosuit. The old man was helping Mom out of hers, and when she was free, she picked him up and hugged him. She hugged Mama, too.

Alvin had been stuck in a lot of places today, but being held by his moms was the best place he could imagine being stuck. Even if Mama was squeezing so hard his cheek was squished into her shoulder.

# The Passion of the Sea

Published January 26, 2018 - StepIntoTheRoad.com

D erek awoke his passion for the sea every time he looked off a boat's deck and into the rolling blue waves. Then he would proceed to vomit. After that, Derek would meander below deck to recover until the excursion was over. He had no logical reason to love the sea. He couldn't explain his feelings for it. In his mind, this was what it meant to have a genuine passion.

People, mostly his exes and shrinks, would relate his love of the sea back to his father. Derek's father was an avid sailor and had won many awards. He sailed his entire adult life, up until the day he traveled through the Strait of Sanmir. Derek's family never learned the details of the sailor's death, but the Coast Guard found shrapnel of the man's beloved boat.

More than anything else Derek wanted to be a sailor. He continuously signed up for sailing classes. He lived in a condo next to a pier so that he heard the ocean at night. It was a method to get over his seasickness, but it just made him nauseous in bed. No matter what Derek did, he couldn't get over his seasickness.

Derek had tried everything. Including, but not limited to, Dramamine, Hypnotherapy, Patches of every color, shape, and size, and bracelets with dirt from twelve different islands. Absolutely nothing worked for him.

While Derek sat on the beach one morning, meditating on the sea and trying to keep his breakfast down, an old woman approached him.

Without waiting for him to acknowledge her, she said, "Young man, I will cure your sickness for you."

She had piqued his interest, but he was dubious as most people should be when offered a cure from a stranger. "How do you know I am sick?" he asked.

"I can see it in your eyes, boy."

Sarcastically he said, "Of course, you can see it in my eyes. I'm looking at the ocean."

"NO!" She said smacking him on the head. "I see the sickness, the longing to love something that your soul is not compatible with. It is common among men," she paused, "and women. I see it for pets, lovers, jobs, and occasionally the sea. However, I have not seen a sickness like yours for many years."

"I'm not sick," he claimed adamantly. It was an impulse response from the dozens of times he had been asked and embarrassed by seamen. "I just get sick every time I look at the sea from an object that isn't dry land."

"That sounds like a sickness to me boy."

He shook his head in protest.

She ignored him, "I'll fix it for you. And you won't even be that cursed afterward."

"What do you mean not even that cursed?"

The old woman shrugged, "I'm a witch I can't give away my cures for free."

"Can I buy you a churro instead?"

"I'm more in the mood for falafels and a gyro," She answered. There's a man, three piers south who makes them just like the old country." She said this with what would be a toothy smile if she had possessed many teeth.

"I'll go get it!" He agreed as he jumped up.

Who knew falafels and a sandwich could solve my problem, he thought as he ran to the restaurant. And even if it didn't work, I could at least say I've tried everything. He rushed to the restaurant a few piers down and bought the woman a meal. To ensure the falafels were fried fresh he paid extra.

He eagerly came back to where he had left her, but there was no woman in sight. All morning he searched, continually tempted by the smell of the fresh food. Slowly the hot lunch got cold but it still tempted him. Lunchtime turned into happy hour then happy hour turned into dinner. His stomach growled, and he wanted to eat the sandwich he had carried all day. Dinner turned to after-dinner drinks, and he had given up hope. Derek sat in the spot where he had started the morning. He had no cure, only a box of cold falafels and a soggy sandwich.

The lunch taunted him all day. Finally, he slammed down on the gyro and the fried chickpea balls thinking to himself, if this is what the food in the old country tasted like I don't blame the lady for coming here.

***

He woke up early for a sailing class. He had, begrudgingly, scheduled it weeks before with the knowledge that he would never have the stomach to sign up on the day of the class. As he headed down to the dock, he pondered what kind of boat he would be on and how rough the weather would be that day.

He got to the dock and saw that it was a small sailboat. Of course, it's a small boat, he thought. Small boats were the worst for him because the wind and waves easily manipulated them. As he waited for others to arrive, he worked to hold his breakfast down despite still being tied to the dock. Once all the other students were there, they set off into open waters.

As they got further and further away from the docks, Derek became more and more worried. However, he did not become any sicker. He was genuinely able to focus on the teacher and not spend his time fighting off early symptoms of puke-your-stomach-up-itis.

As the morning passed the class got to the point where things were hands-on. Derek took to the ropes as a natural. He had learned something from all his classes after all, despite spending most of them below deck. Excited about his new ability Derek took the next course and the one after that. He blew through his certifications and became a genuine sailor.

After years of practice and training, he became a renowned sailor. He won multiple regattas and was often hired to do challenging voyages that most sailors wouldn't dare take on. He experienced strong storms that could only be caused by Neptune's sons bringing home bad test grades three months in a row. All the challenges fueled him and relit his fiery passion for the sea. Not once did Derek become sick.

Over time he got married and had a son named Jacob. He loved his boy more than anything in the world and wanted to share his passion with the kid as soon as he could walk. The problem was that Jacob had seasickness worse than Derek ever had.

In an attempt to help his son with the illness, Derek began to set out falafels and gyros every week. He placed them in the spot where he had first met the old woman. Alas, she never showed. Derek consistently returned to the dock to the sight of seagulls eating away at the meal. Not once did it mysteriously disappear as he had hoped.

His son grew and continued to be sick. Still, the boy had as much interest in the sea as his old man. Derek set off on a trip to sail through the Strait of Sanmir for a lucrative but risky voyage. The area was historically fraught with storms.

One night a storm picked up and Derek, alone on his boat, had to navigate it. He drew in the sails and manipulated his anchor to a position that would help him. As he reached off the side to finagle the anchor onto the ship, he heard a crack of thunder from behind him.

The thunder's crack sounded like a cackle, and it got his attention. He turned, not sure if he should expect someone behind him. Instead, he saw a low mast swing towards him. The wind had caught it, and it was accelerating towards him. Derek jumped out of the way, and the mast swooped over his body. If he hadn't ducked, he would have been thrown from the boat and into the raging waters.

He weathered the storm and spent the rest of the trip in solemn contemplation. Once he returned he tied up his boat to its dock, cleaned out his valuables, and listed the ship for sale.

With the money, he made the trip, and proceeds from the boat he opened a small food stand. It was located near the pier where he lived. Derek and his son Jacob fried falafels and cooked gyros. Their homemade pita was the most popular around. Jacob learned to cook gyros better than his old man could ever hope.

The shop expanded and the family was able to get a seating area and waitstaff. It funded Jacob's college and the two men were always near the sea they loved so much. Jacob went to school and left his father to work alone during the spring and fall.

One cool spring morning Derek saw a woman that looked familiar. He brought her fresh falafels and a warm gyro sandwich before she could order.

He sat down across from her as she snacked on her chickpea snack. A question had been on his mind ever since he survived the Strait of Sanmir. Now, he was finally able to ask her. Derek said, "Why did you let me survive?"

After finishing a slow bite, the woman had somehow lost more teeth in the time since their last meeting, she answered, "Of all your ancestors, you waited the longest time to eat the lunch."

# Crispy Fries

Published May 6, 2022 -
StepIntoTheRoad.com

"ARE YOU HUNGRY?" FLABBERGAST ASKED. "I'M HUNGRY. AFTER WE DROP OFF THIS ONE, WE SHOULD GET SOME FOOD."

"DID YOU LABEL THESE TWO?" THESIS LEANED OVER THE TWO RED-HEADED HUMANS TRYING TO SPOT THE DIFFERENCE.

"NO. THE ONE ON THE LEFT IS FROM 639, AND THE ONE ON THE RIGHT IS FROM 640." FLABBERGAST USED HIS GRAY TENTACLES TO DRAW SERUM OUT OF A VIAL.

"YOUR RIGHT OR MY RIGHT?" THESIS ASKED.

***

Jeremy's head throbbed as he skimmed the emails he'd received overnight. His sleep had been restless and spotted with a vivid dream he could only partially recall. The confusing emails didn't help. They were the standard company updates and notifications about processes that had run successfully overnight. The strange thing about them was that they were all addressed to Leonard.

Leonard was a database admin like him, and he suspected he'd wound up on someone else's laptop, except he'd used his thumbprint to log in, and it was in his cubicle. He was not looking forward to talking to IT about the issue.

"You coming to the stand-up meeting," Nathan asked as he passed Jeremy's desk.

Jeremy's eyebrows raised as he checked his watch. This would be the first time Nathan wasn't late in at least a month.

Soon most of the team trickled in, and they were ready to start their morning check-in meeting, informing each other of their progress to make sure the project moved forward smoothly. Patrick was the last to walk in. Jeremy was surprised at his delay, especially since he typically ran the meeting and was the manager in charge of organizing the whole project.

"Yesterday, I started implementing the UI changes," Nathan said, starting off the meeting. "I'll continue doing that today. No blockers for me."

"I finished writing the script to migrate the data into the warehouse. I will probably spend most of today testing it to fix whatever I missed." Jeremy smiled at the team. Everyone looked back at him, confused.

"What warehouse?" Patrick asked.

"The data warehouse we're building this whole analytics tool on top of," Jeremy said.

"I thought you were going to update the tables I needed for the client's UI changes yesterday. If you didn't do that, I can't finish their request." Nathan said.

Jeremy ran his hands through his thinning red hair. Confusion like this made him anxious. He didn't even know which client Nathan was talking about, but that was the whole point of the stand-up meeting. "If you need some tables updated, I can do that. Just send me what you need."

"I sent it over Monday," Nathan said with little patience. "But I can send it again."

"Wait, what analytic tool are you talking about?" Patrick asked. "You know we're building a custom ticketing system for North Sentry Construction, right?"

That explained the customer that Nathan mentioned. "Yeah, of course," Jeremy said. Stand-ups were supposed to be fast, and he could see this one dragging out. "Just having a foggy morning." He rubbed his head, which still ached.

Patrick didn't press the issue, and soon another team member gave their update. Jeremy understood having to switch projects quickly, but usually, he was notified beforehand.

\*\*\*

ONE OF THE RED-HEADED MEN LYING ON THE BENCH BLINKED AT THESIS. "DID YOU USE THE MUSHALI TO ENSURE THEIR MEMORY WIPE?"

"OF COURSE. I'M NOT AN AMATEUR," FLABBERGAST REPLIED. "IF WE WANT FOOD, WE SHOULD DROP 639 OFF FIRST. THE RESTAURANT NEAR HIS HOUSE HAS THOSE DISGUSTING SOGGY POTATO STICKS."

"HUMANS ARE SO STRANGE IN THEIR EATING PREFERENCES," THESIS SAID AS HE INJECTED MORE SERUM INTO THE VEIN OF THE BLINKING HUMAN. SOON THE MAN RELAXED AND WENT TO SLEEP.

***

"Turns out you did take care of those DB updates yesterday." Nathan leaned on the opening of Jeremy's cubicle.

Jeremy's ticket was still waiting to go through IT, so his morning was slow. The laptop had all his familiar programs installed, but it went against the company's security policy to use someone else's computer, especially since he could log in and run everything.

"Oh good," Jeremy said. "I've been having a slow morning."

"Don't tell Patrick. He's already talking with a customer about another delay."

"Didn't we just start this project?"

"No," Nathan laughed. "With all their minor change requests, it feels like the past five months have been five years."

Jeremy checked his watch. He felt like he'd woken from a coma without anyone telling him how much time had passed. But it was the 22nd, and he remembered wishing his friend a happy birthday yesterday, the 21st.

"Leonard Kowalski?" a young man in khakis and a polo asked. "You have the email issue."

"Anyway, thanks for the table updates. Let me know when you grab lunch." Nathan backed out of the cubicle so the IT guy could come in.

"I'm Jeremy Kowalski. But something happened to my computer, and it keeps saying that Leonard Kowalski is logged in."

"Strange. Seating records say this is Leonard Kowalski's cube. Is Jeremy your middle name or something?"

"No, I don't have a middle name. Parents had a hard enough time agreeing on the first one. Maybe something got messed up in the backend?"

The IT guy opened up his computer and logged in. "I can change your name to Jeremy, but HR will have to approve it. Have you talked to them about it?"

"HR scanned my ID when I got hired here five years ago. They know I'm Jeremy." He tried to keep his tone level, but the whole situation was frustrating.

"Sorry, sir, I am looking to see if there are any changes to your personnel records. Have you left your computer unattended and logged in?"

Jeremy fought the urge to roll his eyes. "I'm certain I haven't." He hadn't left a computer unlocked and unattended since grade school when Thomas used his account to look up pictures of girls in bikinis and then tattled to the teacher.

The IT guy looked at him skeptically but didn't press the issue.

***

"THE CONSCIOUSNESS SIGNALS OF THESE TWO BEINGS ARE QUITE DIFFERENT." THESIS LOOKED AT THE FLOATING BALL OF LIGHT IN FRONT OF HIM. HIS EYESTALKS WIGGLED AROUND TO INSPECT DIFFERENT ANGLES.

"THOSE ARE JUST ANOMALIES. THESE TWO ARE IDENTICAL," FLABBERGAST SAID. "THAT'S WHY I DIDN'T BOTHER LABELING THEM."

"ARE YOU SURE THE ONE ON THE LEFT IS FROM 639? WE NEED TO MAKE SURE THEY GET BACK TO THE RIGHT UNIVERSE."

FLABBERGAST STIFFENED HIS EYESTALKS FOR A MOMENT TO SHOW HIS INDIFFERENCE. "THEIR UNIVERSES ARE BASICALLY THE SAME. THEY WON'T EVEN NOTICE THE DIFFERENCES."

"THIS ONE IS BLINKING AGAIN. ARE YOU SURE YOU USED MUSHALI ON HIM?"

"YES, YES, YES. I WOULD NEVER SKIP THAT STEP," FLABBERGAST SAID.

***

"Frynman's Burgers for lunch?" Nathan asked.

"Definitely," Jeremy agreed. With the chaos of the new project and the mess with his name, he wanted to go somewhere familiar and comforting. He hadn't made any progress with the IT guy, and there wasn't anyone at the company named Leonard Kowalski, aside from his misnaming.

Nathan drove, and they talked about company drama in other departments. Nathan talked about his boyfriend's excitement around their upcoming wedding. Jeremy didn't remember Nathan getting engaged or having a boyfriend. He distinctly remembered meeting his girlfriend at the Christmas party last year. But they were coworkers, and Nathan didn't owe him any updates about his personal life. Nathan was happy, which was all Jeremy wanted for the guy.

Jeremy ordered his favorite: the QED burger. It was a mess of a meal topped with queso, a fried egg, and dill pickles. Nathan ordered Schrodinger's catfish sticks, a meal Jeremy never enjoyed because whoever fried stuff never got anything crispy enough.

"What was all that with the IT guy?"

"I don't know, man." Jeremy rubbed his head. A half dozen Advils hadn't done as much as he'd hoped. "I just hope it gets sorted out soon. Otherwise, I'm not going to get anything done."

"Patrick isn't going to be happy."

"He's not the one getting someone else's emails."

"Yeah, I heard about that. IT has problems but—"

The waiter interrupted with their food.

"I don't know how they messed it up." Jeremy cut into the messy burger. He'd eat the fries later, if at all, since they were always a soggy mess. "But I'm getting this guy Leonard Kowalski's emails."

Nathan gave him a funny look as he bit into his fries. "And you are?"

"Jeremy Kowalski."

"Did you change your name?"

"No! I'm Jeremy Kowalski, I've always been Jeremy Kowalski, and I always will be Jeremy Kowalski!"

"Then I'm sorry I've been calling you Leonard for the past few years."

"You called me Jeremy yesterday. We were on a different project yesterday too. And Patrick showed up to stand-up on time." Jeremy cursed as he took a bite of his fries. They were crisp shoestring fries, precisely what he'd always wanted from Frynman's. He took another bite. "Have these fries always been this crisp?"

"Yeah, that's half the reason we come here."

"No, we come here for the burgers, and I've never seen you order anything other than the Quantum Spice Burger."

"Do you need to go to a doctor? I'm not trying to be rude, but you sound crazy."

"I feel crazy! How many kids do I have?"

"Two."

"That's good; the girls are still in my life."

"I thought you had two sons."

Jeremy dropped the fries out of his hand and stood up. The chair's metal frame clinked to the ground as he paced back and forth, muttering the most elaborate curses he knew.

"Leonard—" Nathan started.

Jeremy gave him a look like a bull facing down a matador.

"Jeremy," Nathan said, "sit down. It's going to be okay."

Jeremy saw the wait staff and other customers looking at him. He picked his chair off the ground and sat down. He hated causing a scene.

"I had a dream last night," Jeremy whispered, "and I'm starting to think it happened. But it's not going to make me sound sane."

"If sharing will make you feel better, let's hear it. Especially if it keeps me from going back to making those UI changes."

***

"One down, one to go," Flabbergast said as the tractor beam dropped the human off in the bed where they'd initially abducted him.

Thesis flipped some switches on the ship's console, and they flashed into a parallel universe.

"Mrhm mrrm brm," someone said from the back of the ship.

"They don't usually wake up this much," Thesis said. "If we give him much more sleeping serum, he will have a splitting headache tomorrow."

"Well, we've got to put him to sleep. Otherwise, he'll start thrashing around and mess up the beam."

"When they have mushali in their system, they sleep better." Thesis rearranged his gills and shongdin to indicate he doubted Flabbergast's statement.

"I definitely used the mushali on one of them."

"THEY BOTH NEED IT!" THESIS THREW HALF HIS TENTACLES
INTO THE AIR. "WHAT ARE WE SUPPOSED TO DO NOW? WHAT
IF HE LANDS IN THE WRONG UNIVERSE, REMEMBERS OUR FACES,
THEN REPORTS US TO THE GALACTIC COUNCIL?"

"WE ALL LOOK THE SAME TO THEM," FLABBERGAST ASSURED
HIM. "BESIDES, THIS SPECIES ISN'T A PART OF THE COUNCIL.
WHICH IS WHY WE EXPERIMENT ON THEM."

"THAT STILL DOESN'T MAKE IT RIGHT," THESIS SAID AS HE
INJECTED SLEEPING SERUM INTO THE HUMAN'S BONY ARM.

\*\*\*

When Jeremy finished telling Nathan about his abduction dream,
both had finished their food and paid their bill.

"Well, that didn't make you sound any saner," Nathan said. "And
if what you say is true, what are you going to do? Find this Galactic
Council they mentioned?"

Jeremy buried his head in his hands. He'd been mulling this over
since Nathan mentioned his kids had changed. Telling anyone else
would make him sound crazier and land him in a mental hospital or
as a test subject. And after last night, he didn't want to experience that
again.

"Maybe I go on an epic space adventure to take on this advanced
alien civilization and force them to return me to my original galaxy?"
Jeremy laughed at how ridiculous it sounded.

"They pay us well... but not that well," Nathan said with a smile.

"I just have to go back to work and hope Leonard does the same.
Take care of his family and hope he takes care of mine."

"Patrick will be glad to hear that. We're certainly not going to be able to finish this North Sentry thing on time without you."

As they left, Jeremy hoped that Leonard's database structure wasn't as messy as previous data structures he'd previously cleaned up.

# Oily Salesmen and Snakes

Published March 30, 2018 -
StepIntoTheRoad.com

L arry and Harry sat alone in their pharmacy. It had been days
since a customer came in and this wasn't a new problem.

Harry sat with his cowboy boots resting on the wooden counter.
He said, "Ain't nobody been 'round for days."

"I know," Larry the pharmacist said picking at his teeth with a
splinter of wood.

"What about Brenda, she came in a few days ago for cough syrup.
She should need more by now, right?"

Larry shrugged, "Don't know if she's going to be coming back. Her
husband has been trying to get her off that stuff."

"The bastard," Harry cursed as he spat his dip into a spittoon.
"What about..."

Larry cut him off knowing what he was going to say. "Nope, Eli
doesn't need anything for his foot anymore. It healed a month ago."

Harry started spinning his knife between his fingers, bored. Then the bell hanging over the door rang. Both men came to attention to see who just walked in.

"How can we help you," Larry said from behind the counter.

The man who walked didn't live in their small town and was a stranger to them. The man wore polished black boots, a dark ten-gallon hat, and a smooth leather vest. He was slick as a trout fresh from the river. The man appeared young in complexion, but the grey hair that popped out under his hat proved differently.

"Actually, I was wondering if you boys needed my help," He said with a smile.

Larry looked at the man confused. Harry, not one to keep his mouth shut when he had a thought, said "And how do you reckon that?"

"Well you're running an apothecary, and I happen to be selling medicine." The man produced a small unmarked vial of golden liquid. "This is oil for your skin. It keeps you looking young, and it clears any blemishes or scars you have. That is if you use it regularly."

Larry picked up the vial, opened the top by popping off the cork, and took a whiff of the liquid. "It does all that?" he asked.

The stranger gestured at his clear complexion, "Look at me, I use it every day."

"What is it exactly?" Larry asked as he dropped a bit of it on his hand, put the vial down, and rubbed it in. Harry snatched the vial from the counter and investigated it. Harry was one for fighting and had plenty of scars to show for it. Most notably the one on his right forearm.

"It's oil of the rattlesnake. But don't worry, it's not venomous. It's neutralized to the point that the chemicals will only help your skin and won't hurt you. Are you fine gentlemen interested in buying some?"

Harry looked at his business partner and raised a single eyebrow. Larry shrugged and looked at the traveler, "What's the catch? Why don't you sell it yourself?"

The man frowned and began to explain his situation, "You see, I'm not from these parts, and the oil only works if you use it regularly. I can't stick around here for long enough to sell them all. But I have a cartload of them. I'm willing to sell all of it to you. Then you will be able to sell them to your customers regularly, and they'll actually get results. Something this valuable would be worth a shiny dime, but I'll be selling them to you for less than a nickel each. That is if you're willing to take up this once-in-a-lifetime offer. If you don't take me up I'll just sell it to the next pharmacy I come by."

The two men looked at each other. Then they looked at the man across the counter, "One second." Larry said before his partner could open his mouth and ruin the deal. Then they disappeared into the empty storage room to confer.

***

Larry put down the last crate of snake oil and wiped the sweat off his forehead with his white apron. After Harry convinced Larry to use the last of their cash to buy the oil the two men did some quick negotiation with the salesman and tested the product themselves. After the deal was done, they began the laborious task of unloading the product into their storage room.

"It will pay for itself in no time," Harry assured his partner who was staring at the room filled with boxes. Harry smiled a big crooked grin at his friend. "This," he gestured to the room full of boxes, "this is going to make us rich. This place is going to become the only pharmacy anyone in this town comes to."

"We're the only pharmacy in town," Larry pointed out. "But I agree, this stuff is going to be all anyone talks about for the next few months."

They stayed up all night labeling the ointment, "Larry and Harry's Miracle Elixir." Under the name, the label read, "Guaranteed to fix warts, scars, and all blemishes of the skin."

The next day the two men stood on the porch of their store and sold their new product on the street. By noon they had sold ten vials, and by the end of the day, they had sold the the last of their first crate.

They walked back inside their store and examined the dozens of crates still filling their stock room. Larry frowned and the unsold merchandise.

"Don't worry," Harry said reading his partner's expression better than he ever read a book. "We'll sell even more tomorrow. Not to mention in less than a week everyone will be coming back for more. And they'll be telling their friends too," Harry beamed.

"If you say so. What do we do if we run out of this supply?"

"Let's worry about that problem when it arrives. Look at this," Harry said showing Larry his arm. "You think this scar looks like it's clearing up?"

Larry examined the scar that Harry was showing him. "I guess so," Larry said with a shrug.

"Yeah, I think so too. I'm gonna take a bottle home and use it tonight. It'll be gone by next week at this rate.

\*\*\*

A week later Harry showed his partner the improvement of the scar. Larry hadn't noticed much change and returned his attention to the store's account books. They weren't promising either. Sales of the product had spiked at the beginning but quickly decreased. The men were only selling one or two bottles a day, and none of them were to repeat customers.

The bell over the door rang for the first time that day. Larry's focus on the books disappeared. Harry spat out some chew and stood up as the town gossip, Mrs. Belford, waddled into the store. She was short in stature but carried the weight of a woman twice her height. Her body had multiple moles and pimples. There was also a notable wart on her cheek. She was a prime customer for the two men's ointment. They had sold her a vial on day one.

"How can we help you, ma'am," Larry asked with a smile.

"You can help me by refunding the money you stole from me by selling me this useless vial." She slammed a small empty glass container onto the counter.

Harry stepped in, "What exactly are you accusing us of?"

"Being sham medicine men, first of all! Then false advertising too," she said aggressively to the man. "I've been using it for two weeks now, and this big ol' wart has not gone away." She gestured at the big hairy wart on her cheek. "I use it every day, twice a day, and nothing has happened. It hasn't even gotten smaller."

Harry pulled his sleeve over the scar on his arm and then said, "Well, that is a pretty big wart. Our elixir only works if you use it for a long time. If you would like you can buy some more for us."

"Oh and throw good money after bad?" She said with a scoff. "I want my dime back, or I will tell the whole town that you're scamming people out of their money."

Knowing that Mrs. Belford was likely to tell the whole town regardless of the men's reaction to the situation, Larry reached into the cash register and produced a small dime. "Here you go Mrs. Belford," he said, "I'm sorry the ointment didn't work for you. I'd be happy to serve you with any other medicine you need in the future."

She snorted and began to waddle back out of the store.

"Some people just won't use medicine like they're prescribed," Harry asked.

Larry didn't have a chance to explain it to his thick-skulled friend because for the second time that day, the bell on the door rang, and someone walked in.

Unfortunately, it wasn't a customer but the mailman. "How's it going today, Gene?" Larry asked politely.

The young man shrugged and handed the men a small letter then quickly left. "Who's it from?" Harry said looking at the envelope.

As the ring from the door faded into the room Larry answered, "The bank." He hesitated, then opened it up to read it. Harry was illiterate so he had to give the synopsis to him. "They say they're going to foreclose on our store because we are behind on our payments." He said giving his partner a worried look.

"Well then let's pay them," Harry said matter of factly.

Larry rolled his eyes, "We can't. We spent all of our cash on the oil."

Harry frowned, "Well then we just need to sell more. Let's go back out to the streets and start selling like mad."

Before Larry could argue that this was what they had been doing to no avail the little bell over the door rang. The two men looked to see what fresh hell had walked in for them this time.

Harry was pleased to see the young schoolteacher Mary Ann Lewis walk through the door. She was remarkably beautiful, new to town, and single. Because of this Harry immediately offered her help.

"What brings you all the way to our side of town?" Harry asked. The schoolteacher lived with the Bronsons who were her host family.

She explained her problem to the smiling man, "Well you see, I have been using this elixir of yours on my neck for a while now, and I haven't seen any improvements." She gestured at the large wine-colored birthmark that was on her neck. It was the only blemish on her healthy body. "I've had it since I was a kid but I've always hated it. I was hoping this stuff would get rid of it. Unfortunately, I'm not having success with your stuff. Has anyone else complained?"

Larry began to explain, but Harry cut him off. "Mary Ann, you're the first person who has come in with this whole problem. How much have you used? Do you need to buy more?" Then he took a look at her neck, "Larry do you think she should increase the dosage? Why don't we send you home with two bottles and you can use one in the morning and one in the afternoon."

"I don't really think that's a good idea," the woman said nervously, "Mr. Bronson and his wife think I should demand a refund but I was just curious if I was the only one with the problem. And if I came home with twice as much, they would surely throw a fit."

Larry stepped in and took Harry's focus off the young woman. "You know it doesn't work for some people because of their blood. Here's your dime back, we're so sorry we couldn't help you. Of course, if you think there's anything we could help you with, we'd be happy to."

"Thank you, Mr. Larry," Mary Ann said politely. "I will keep you in mind." And with that, she left the store.

As the ring of the bell came to a silence Larry looked at his partner, "We have a problem."

"What?" Harry asked still staring out the window at the young woman.

"The ointment doesn't work." Larry said, "And we have an entire stock room full of it. Not to mention, we don't have money for the bank this month which means we won't have a store next week."

Harry shrugged turning away from the window once Mary Ann was out of site. Addressing his partner he asked, "What do you mean it doesn't work? It's been working on me. Those people just don't have the right blood for it. You said so yourself."

"Harry you moron, I made that up so Marry Ann wouldn't feel bad," as he questioned why he had ever gone into business with someone with the brains of a mule. But what's done was done. All Larry could do now was try to save his failing store. The store he always dreamed of starting. All he wanted to do was bring healthy remedies to the people of his town.

He grabbed five vials of their bogus oil from the shelves and walked back to the workbench where he made medicine for their now dwindling number of customers.

"What're you doing?" Harry asked in a long drawl.

"Fixing this," Larry said without looking up from the mortar and pestle he was working with.

***

Larry worked long hours for the next three days trying to find some way he could use the snake oil for a profit. After running out of lamp oil late one night, he dumped a small vial into his old soot-covered lamp. The oil worked but that was the only viable use he had found so far. Lamp oil was cheap compared to what they paid for the ointment, and they would never make any money selling it like that.

On the fourth day, Harry came in and asked his partner, "How's it coming?"

"Mrn Mrinet," Larry said with his mouth full.

Harry's interest was peaked. He looked at his partner across the store and saw the man foaming at the mouth. "Lord almighty, what have you done!?" Harry exclaimed at his ravenous-looking partner.

Larry spat the foam into the nearby spittoon and smiled at his friend. There was a little bit of foam left around his mouth, "What do you think?"

"About what?"

"My teeth. Do they look whiter?"

Harry inspected the man's mouth. Larry had never chewed much tobacco. Harry had to admit that the man's teeth did look a little cleaner.

"I've been working on a new use for the snake oil and I think I've got something. I mixed it with some other ingredients and a little mint, and I made a paste. You stick it on your finger and rub it on your teeth to clean them. I think it will be better for your gums and will at least clean the tobacco stains off of your teeth." He offered a small bowl of paste to his partner. Harry looked at the bowl and then at his smiling partner. "Come on give it a try," Larry encouraged.

The man stuck his finger in the bowl and doubtfully rubbed the paste over his front teeth. He moved his finger away and looked at the small mirror sitting on Larry's desk. Sure enough, they were significantly whiter than the teeth around them. "My breath tastes better too," Harry remarked.

Larry nodded, "It's something I've been working on for a while. But I've never had anything to bind the basic materials together. Then I tried the oil, and it held them together."

"Do you know how much people would pay for better-looking teeth?" Harry asked after he finished rubbing all the rest of his crooked teeth with his finger.

"I'll be happy if we can cover rent this month," Larry admitted.

"Make some more of this," Harry proclaimed, "We will be doing more than just breaking even. We'll be the most popular pharmacy in town."

Larry didn't point out that they were still the only pharmacy for miles.

***

Three days later most of the vials of oil had been converted into paste. Harry and Larry once again stood on the street in front of their shop. It was a beautifully sunny day, and the town was bustling. The men started hawking their goods, but no one showed any interest in their paste. Eventually, Miss Mary Ann walked by, and Harry was able to stop her to talk. Not because he was particularly charming but because she was uncannily polite.

"Mary Ann come try this new paste for your teeth that Larry invented," He uncorked the vial and held it under her nose. Her eyes perked up at the mint smell, so she approached the booth.

"How does it work?" She asked out of curiosity.

"You simply put a little bit on your finger and rub it on your teeth," Larry explained with a genuine smile. "You'll be able to see the difference in the mirror as soon as you're done."

Mary Ann dipped a thin finger into the bottle and began to rub it on her teeth. She had never chewed tobacco and that was one of the reasons she was so pretty. She smiled at the mirror and then frowned. "I'm sorry Mr. Larry, but I don't see much of a difference."

Larry looked at her teeth and had to admit that she was right. It had a dramatic effect on Harry because of his poor hygiene, but this woman didn't need their product. "Well I'm sure it worked, just because you don't have mud all over you doesn't mean you don't need a weekly bath," Larry said with a smile.

"Can we interest you in a bottle?" Harry jumped in eagerly in an attempt to close the sale.

"I'm sorry, I can't afford it and if I'm frank Mr. and Mrs. Bronson would have a fit if I bring home another one of your gimmicks," she said. Only added, "No offense," after noticing Larry's hurt expression.

Harry went to open his mouth to disagree, but Larry cut him off, "It's fine, I hope you enjoy the fresh breath for a while, and if you ever change your mind we will be here." Larry lied knowing that if they didn't sell enough bottles today they'd be foreclosed on.

An hour later, with no bites, Mrs. Belford waddled past their porch. Harry stopped her to pitch the product. Before Harry could finish the pitch, Mrs. Belford cut him off, "I don't care if your medicine makes me as fast as a Jackrabbit I'm not buying another thing from your store ever again." She then barreled past Harry and continued to the town's general store.

For the rest of the day, the two men couldn't interest a single client. Almost no one would stop, and those few who did refused to buy it even after seeing the improvement. Some of them had remarkable results, but they didn't feel like it was because of the paste. Harry got frustrated and nearly started a fight with a rancher, but Larry was able to talk the two men down.

The sun began to set, and the luckless shop owners started to pack up their paste. "Maybe we'll have better luck tomorrow," Harry said.

Larry stayed silent, knowing tomorrow would never come, as they packed up the final pieces of their setup. A suited man in a bowler hat came up to the porch of their shop with some papers in his hand. "How can we help you, Mr. Wilson," Harry asked. Larry perked up after hearing the banker's name. He felt his stomach somersault.

"Unfortunately for you, I'm here to make sure that you've packed everything up and are ready to move out by tomorrow. We have a new tenant taking over your storefront soon."

"Excuse me!" Harry exclaimed in shock.

Larry stepped in and addressed the issue before a fight started. "I'm sorry Harry, I didn't want to tell you but today's the day they set to foreclose on us. I was hoping we could sell enough paste to turn the budget around, but the paste isn't selling. We have to pack up and move out tonight."

The bowler-hatted banker nodded his head in agreement, "Sorry to do it to you boys, but it seems the town isn't quite ready for a pharmacy. Especially one that's selling sham potions." The man picked up the last vial of paste that was sitting out. "But tell me, I'm curious, what did you come up with this week?"

"It's soap for your teeth," Harry explained quickly and frustrated.

The man simply laughed, "No one would put soap on their teeth. And even if they did why would they want to?" Henry began to explain, but the banker waved his hand dismissing the man, "I don't need to hear whatever excuse you've made up. Although I'm sure, it's convincing. I just want your stuff out of the shop and for you to go home. Better yet leave this town and go somewhere people still trust your fake medicine and scams. But in this town, I don't think you'll ever be able to sell anything ever again, even if you had water from the fountain of youth."

Larry's heart sank. He had worked hard to keep his pharmacy afloat and give the town something he thought they needed. But they no longer trusted him. After a day of being rejected by the town for his fantastic new problem, he wasn't ready to fight to stay in the store. Without saying anything to Harry he put the last bottle of paste in the trash instead of the crate it belonged in.

## Also By Nicholas Licalsi

### Path of the Bearers and Other Stories

An AI with the potential to predict the future must uncover its creator's inexplicable disappearance. A scientist must reveal the limitations of his high profile project to while his investor takes them on a joyride through an asteroid field. A writer travels to a pocket dimension to find time to write, but something sinister follows.

Visit seedy space station bars, distant planets where dormant aliens rest. One wrong decision could ruin humanity's chances of surviving among the stars.

This book is your portal to explore the cosmos and beyond...
https://books2read.com/PathOfTheBearersAndOtherStories

## Bleeding Rock

Mauve, a talented mechanic, always dreamed of leaving her satellite home. So she didn't think twice before signing up for a routine planetary survey.

Mauve awakes from the landing hanging upside down. Clearly something went wrong. She will need all her mechanical knowledge to get the mission back on track.

But the crash landing is only the start of her troubles.

With her AI assistant Mauve must use everything she discovers on this alien world to escape it.

If you enjoy science fiction exploration stories with elements of horror then you'll love Bleeding Rock!

https://books2read.com/BleedingRock

## A Trial of Rock and Rope

Upon his death, Ferrun Monteiro wakes up in the afterlife. Instead of building paradise the gods have designed a challenge.

To escape the afterlife Ferrun must reach the top of a mountain with a boulder tied to his ankle.

Yet not a single soul has completed this seemingly simple trial.

Unperturbed, Ferrun faces the god's challenge head on. Follow him on his odyssey through the afterlife.

If you enjoy dreaming about the afterlife, you'll enjoy A Trial of Rock and Rope.

https://books2read.com/ATrialOfRockAndRope

# About the Author

Nicholas Licalsi was born and raised outside of Fort Worth, in the beautiful but backwards state of Texas. Growing up, he was fascinated with science fiction and fantasy. This interest led to pursuing a degree in engineering and participating in multiple robotics competitions. After a successful enough career in software development Nicholas spends his time trying to trick his overactive imagination into paying the bills while he satiates his dog's need to be pet.

**You can connect with me at:** https://stepintotheroad.com

**Get updates about my upcoming books at:** https://stepintoth eroad.com/signup